OATH

Look for other books
by Chuck Black

The Kingdom Series
Kingdom's Dawn
Kingdom's Hope
Kingdom's Edge
Kingdom's Call
Kingdom's Quest
Kingdom's Reign

The Knights of Arrethtrae
Sir Kendrick and the Castle of Bel Lione
Sir Bentley and Holbrook Court
Sir Dalton and the Shadow Heart
Lady Carliss and the Waters of Moorue
Sir Quinlan and the Swords of Valor
Sir Rowan and the Camerian Conquest

The Starlore Legacy
Nova
Flight
Lore
Oath
Merchant
Reclamation
Creed
Journey
Crucible
Covenant
Revolution
Maelstrom

www.ChuckBlack.com

THE STARLORE LEGACY

OATH

EPISODE **FOUR**

CHUCK BLACK

PERFECT
PRAISE
PUBLISHING

Oath

Cover design ©2021 by Elena Karoumpali
Tech Drawing Illustrations ©2022 by Chuck Black and ©2022 by
Reese Black

Published by Perfect Praise Publishing
Williston, North Dakota

ISBN 978-1-7359061-7-1

Printed in the United States of America

Library of Congress Control Number: 2022904398

Contents

Prologue - Returning Home   9

Chapter 1 - Empty   17

Chapter 2 - Betrayed   33

Chapter 3 - To Build a World   51

Chapter 4 - The Zeal of Ell Yon   69

Chapter 5 - The Acumen of a Navi   78

Chapter 6 - Not Alone   88

Chapter 7 - The Battle for Rayl   100

Chapter 8 - The Victory Gala   116

Chapter 9 - Judgment   130

Chapter 10 - The Empire of Zar   139

Chapter 11 - Captives   149

Chapter 12 - Simulations That Kill   164

Chapter 13 - The Trials   178

Chapter 14 - The Wrath of Zar   192

Chapter 15 - War in the Ruah   201

Chapter 16 - Oath of Ell Yon   216

Chapter 17 - Revelation   223

Chapter 18 - The Last Goodbye   231

PROLOGUE

Returning Home

B rae Thornton was lost in thought—reflections of the curved windscreen danced off her cheeks as the world outside flashed by. It had been months since she'd been home. Having just finished her third year at the astrotech institute in Jalem, she was a different person than when she had left. As a fully qualified astrotech, she could now apply for the astrotech master program. From her early childhood years, it was the stars that had drawn her to the astrotech order. She couldn't deny that the adventure-filled stories her father had told her certainly were a motivating impact on this decision, but she was quite convinced that even without the stories, she would have ended up an astrotech master. Something deep inside her ached to know what, why, and how such incredible phenomena in space existed. Her quest to find those answers was expensive, however, especially since the Morian occupiers of Rayl required a twenty percent tribute fee. She shook her head just thinking about it. The Morian Empire was a strong boot on the neck of Rayl, and there was nothing the Rayleans could do about it, at least not now. There were many that claimed the ancient Oracle and Navi prophecies predicted that Ell Yon's Commander would arrive and lead a rebellion against the Morian oppression on their homeworld, but her father disregarded such fanciful interpretations. Her thoughts then turned to Elias. How could her father afford to pay for her studies on the wages of a geo-mapping surveyor? She missed him.

It was a thirty-minute flight by way of a hover ferry out to her home. She broke from her distant thoughts long enough to be enchanted with the warm memories of her childhood country life as the hills and trees beckoned her. Without realizing it, her lips had turned upward into a smile of remembrance.

"I'll walk from here," Brae said to the ferry pilot.

The craft slowed and dropped to the ground. "Are you sure?" he asked. "We're still two miles away from the drop point."

"Yeah, I'm sure," Brae replied. "Would you please take my luggage the rest of the way for me?"

"You paid for it, so sure. No problem."

Brae thanked the man, then started off into the country to visit some of her favorite places. Nearly an hour later, satiated by the embrace of the land that had been her kingdom as a child, she jumped over the last rock wall that bordered their home.

"How was your walk?" Elias's voice called from beneath the sprawling tree that had been home to many hours together.

"Dad!" Brae exclaimed, running the last hundred feet to greet her father.

Brae wrapped her arms around Elias's neck. There was something about Dad's embrace that healed the ache in her heart.

"Oh, Dad...I've missed you!"

Elias held her out at arm's length. "And I you, sweetheart. How are you?"

Brae smiled from ear to ear. "Great...now. This last quarter was grueling. I'm glad to be done for a couple of months."

"I'm sure," Elias said, wrapping an arm around her as they turned and walked to the bench beneath the tree. "But in a couple of weeks when you find out you've been accepted into the master program, you'll be itching to get back to your studies."

Brae smiled. "You mean, *if* I get into the program."

"Oh, I have no doubt about that," Elias countered.

Brae filled her lungs with fresh autumn air. "Well, for now, it just really feels good to be home."

"And it's really good to have you here."

Elias and Brae sat on the comfortable weathered bench. She leaned back, closed her eyes and drank in the sweet fresh air of the country.

"When your luggage arrived, I figured you were close behind, so I poured you a glass of bossberry tea." Elias handed Brae a glass of the pale pink liquid, condensation beading on all sides of the container's cold surface. "But I thought you were arriving yesterday."

Brae took a long satisfying drink of the sweet tea, enjoying the cool sensation it created all the way down her throat.

"I wanted to attend the unveiling of the newest Protector at Sovereign's Sanctum yesterday." She looked at her father, waiting for a reaction. "They have six Protectors now."

Elias nodded, saying nothing.

"The Builders of the Protectors looked pretty pleased, and so did the Keepers." Brae added, knowing this would provoke some sort of response.

"I'll bet they did," Elias finally said with a subtle smirk on his face. "Did you have a Keeper scan you?"

Brae swiped down her glass squeegeeing a portion of the condensation from one side.

"Yes, I did," she answered, looking down at the grass beneath her feet. "And yes, they charged me to do so."

Elias huffed. "Hypocrites. They abuse the Protectors to gain status and wealth for themselves. I'd like to scan them! I'm surprised the Protectors even allow such a thing from those vipers."

Elias stopped himself, exhaled, then smiled. "And did the Keeper have any great words of wisdom for you?"

Brae looked up, returning the smile. "No. But he looked surprised. Made a comment about having never seen such a low percentage of Deitum Prime in one my age before."

Elias put an arm around Brae, pulling her in for a quick hug. She leaned in, loving the feeling of her dad's strong arm around her.

"Did you ask to don the Protector?" Elias asked, letting her go.

Brae jerked her head back. "What? No...of course not! Why would I do that?"

"It's the right of every Raylean, if they so choose to," Elias replied. "The Protectors are not just for the Builders and the Keepers. They're for all people."

"But except for scanning Deitum Prime levels, the Protectors have gone silent...everyone knows that. Not even the Keepers hear Ell Yon anymore."

"Hmm," was Elias's reply. "And by the way, there aren't just six Protectors."

Brae looked over at her father. "You speak of the fabled missing seventh Protector."

Elias raised an eyebrow, glancing toward her out of the corner of his eye. "Some say it was the original Protector given by Ell Yon to Navi Starlore thousands of years ago."

Brae shrugged her shoulders. "I guess we'll never know."

Elias didn't reply—he just slowly nodded.

For the next few days, Brae and Elias allowed themselves the freedom to just enjoy each other's company, often leaving chores for another day so they could soak up the minutes spent together. One evening, Elias tapped on Brae's door as she was preparing to end the day.

"Come in," she called.

Elias stepped through the door as it slid away.

"I just wanted to check on you to see if you needed anything," Elias said.

Brae pulled her knees up to her chest and patted the bed. Elias smiled, then sat down at the foot of her bed.

"I told you a lot of stories sitting right here." His gentle eyes warmed with fond memories.

"Yes, you did," Brae replied. "And it seems to me that you never told the endings to them."

Elias laughed. "Is there ever really an end to any story?" he asked.

Brae's smile slowly faded. "Maybe not. Is that why, Dad? Is it because there really isn't an end to those stories or is it something else?"

Some of the delight in Elias's eyes dimmed. "What do you mean?"

Brae hesitated. "Never mind."

Elias tilted his head. "What's on your mind, Brae?"

Brae squirmed. "Dad...I'm not sixteen anymore. I'm different...I didn't realize how much becoming an adult changes a person."

"Yes..." Elias prompted.

Brae fiddled with the braid that hung over the front of her shoulder then looked at Elias. "At the institute, no one believes the legends like you taught me to. It's been hard." Brae bit her lip, closely watching his reaction.

One eyebrow raised as Elias gazed back at Brae. "Legends?"

Brae's shoulders sank. "As a child, the stories you told filled me with wonder and delight. What child wouldn't be taken away with such tales. But now, as an adult, the galaxy looks different, Dad...much different."

Elias was still, silently waiting. Brae wanted to stop...to retract each word she'd just spoken, but this was a conversation that she knew was coming. The realist part of her was quickly overtaking any fanciful dreams that lingered from her childhood. It was a natural consequence of the institute and her studies there. She didn't want to hurt her dad but...

"I'm sorry. I've just grown up, and I see things as they really are now."

Brae could hardly stand the sadness that had settled in the eyes of her father.

"Many at the institute argue that there is absolutely no scientific evidence that the Immortals even exist, let alone the dimension of the Ruah you speak of. It's been nearly 500 years since the last reported appearance of anything that even remotely resembles Sovereign Ell Yon being involved in the lives of the Rayleans—five hundred years! Stories like that are often embellished in just a few years." Brae tried to stop, but the last eighteen months of her processing these thoughts had a momentum she couldn't seem to control. "Where is he, Dad? Where is Ell Yon?"

The former delight in Elias's face was now completely absent. "Why did you go see the unveiling of the new Protector then?" he asked.

Brae slowly shook her head. "I don't know...I guess to see if anything had changed." Her head dropped lower. "Even you have said the Protectors are being used to manipulate and control the people. Maybe they're just relics that have enticed grand stories people wanted to hear. Honestly, even the Keepers of the Protectors seem cynical. I think you're right...they're a bunch of hypocrites."

Brae looked at Elias, his eyes ripe with the pain of abandonment. She reached for his arm.

"I'm sorry, Dad, please don't be angry with me. I've been struggling with this for a long time. I just don't know how to reconcile those grand stories you told me when I was a child with what the institute is teaching."

Elias seemed frozen...stunned. Brae could hardly bear it. She scooted next to him and leaned on his strong shoulder.

After a long while, Elias cleared his throat. "There's a reason I never told you the end of the story, Brae." Elias's voice quavered. "Would you like to hear it now?"

Brae sighed. Had she ruined the next two months home with her father?

"Sure," Brae said, hoping her tone didn't sound indifferent. "I'd like to hear it," she added, trying to band-aid her previous response.

Elias turned to look at her. His gaze alarmed Brae. Behind the edges of sadness that laced the corners of his eyes, the passion inside them was undaunted. This conversation had changed them...both of them. No longer was there the tender look that had before accompanied his hours of storytelling. Brae responded, leaning back against the headboard of her bed. She would listen one more time.

"As in the days of the flight from Jypton, the people of Rayl were prone to wander from the ways of Sovereign Ell Yon. From generation to generation, the hearts of the people grew weak in their faith in him. It was this struggle that set the destiny of Daeson and Raviel Starlore...a destiny that followed them through the annals of time..."

CHAPTER

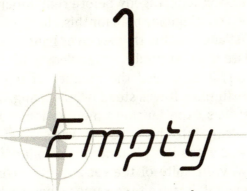

1

Empty

Daeson stood looking at the empty space where Raviel had just been, his heart shattered once more. Her Talon lay at his feet while a few fragments of her outer clothing sifted down to the ground like leaves falling from an autumn tree. Daeson slowly sank to his knees, despair fully swallowing him.

"Raviel, I'm sorry."

It wasn't reasonable for Daeson to think her demise was his fault, but reason didn't matter. He couldn't escape the condemning feeling that she was suffering because of him, and it hurt more than he could bear. The quantum phase anomaly had taken her from him...from right before his eyes. Pushing the Protector onto her arm just before she had vanished was the only thing he could think of to help her. The implications of that single action hadn't even begun to sink in yet. If he were honest with himself, it terrified him. Had he condemned the Raylean people to a future without the Sovereign's voice? Worse yet, was Ell Yon angry with him for banishing the Protector to the same fate as Raviel? What would this all mean? It was an instinctual reaction...an impulse to do whatever was possible to save the one he loved...his bonded Raviel.

Daeson wasn't sure how long he'd wallowed in the mire of despondent tragedy before remembering they had made a contingency plan for this. He glanced down at his wrist and saw the thin receiver band that Avidan had created. Quantumly entangled with Raviel's transmitter, it displayed the number of months she was time-slipping. It was steadily increasing...*22...23...*

Raviel was experiencing time dilation that would push her years into the future. It was surreal to think that she was actually still standing in front of him, just inches away. In spite of the recurring horror of this quantum event, it wasn't the same as before. He knew exactly where she was, when she was, and that she wasn't experiencing the ice-cold deathly grip of space. He began to formulate a plan, one that would ensure Raviel's return to normal spacetime was safe. He carefully carved out a circle in the ground around the exact spot where Raviel had stood, the tender blades of spring grass still bent and crushed by her former presence.

"I will keep you safe, my love, and I will come for you...I promise!"

Despite Daeson's cautious optimism in mitigating Raviel's spacetime demise, there was a deeper looming dread that he could not escape. He had just sent the Protector into the future thereby condemning the burgeoning race of Rayleans to a perilous struggle on a new planet with countless enemies and no connection to the mighty Sovereign Ell Yon. Although Daeson had just led his people to victory over the Reekojans, thereby allowing the Rayleans to make their claim on this world as their own, the Protector was the affirming evidence of Ell Yon's promise to always be with them.

Daeson's selfish act to protect Raviel might very well put the entire population at grave risk.

He disappeared from everyone for the rest of the day, including Tig, Kyrah, and Rivet, unable to reveal his folly yet. At first, Daeson didn't even dare let his mind absorb the full impact his action might have, but as the day passed, and he rested his head upon his pillow at night, overwhelming fear nearly swallowed him. Was Ell Yon furious with him? How could he lead the people if he was willing to jeopardize their entire future for his own bonded's sake? Through the course of this sleepless night Daeson came to the full understanding of his grave mistake as the faces of hundreds of thousands of Rayleans swept across his mind in a collage of soul-crushing guilt. In addition, without his connection to Ell Yon, he had never felt so alone in all his life. What would he do now? What *could* he do now? He remembered the face of Ell Yon the day the Immortal had bequeathed the Protector to him. Something deep and sacrificial laced his noble face as he handed it to Daeson.

"Now it begins!" The Immortal's words echoed over and over in his mind. Had he just ended it? He considered flying to Galeo, the place Ell Yon had entrusted Daeson with the Protector. Dare he ask for another? Was there another? Daeson felt like a complete idiot.

"I'm so sorry, Sovereign," he whispered in the still, dark night. "I was desperate to help her...to help your servant. What should I have done?" He asked the questions, but there was no voice to respond.

The following morning, Tig and Kyrah found Daeson sitting in the captain's seat on the empty bridge of the Liberty. They were eager to set the formation of a new world in motion. Tig stopped short at the pain he saw in Daeson's eyes. Without a word having been spoken, he knew what had happened and set a gentle hand on Daeson's shoulder.

"I'm sorry, my friend."

Daeson slowly lifted his gaze upward, eyes red with sorrow. He struggled to speak his error.

"Is the receiver tracking her?" Kyrah asked.

Daeson looked down at the wristband...219.

"Yes," came his nearly silent whisper. He glanced from Kyrah to Tig. "But I've committed the most grievous of errors."

Tig's brow furrowed, questioning. Daeson took his left hand and slid up the sleeve on his right arm. Tig and Kyrah both became stolid. Daeson's eyes filled with tears.

"It's unforgivable...I was desperate to help her...an impulse decision."

Tig swallowed. Neither he nor Kyrah dared even offer any comfort. How could they?

"Would Ell Yon bestow another Protector?" Tig asked solemnly.

Daeson closed his eyes, reliving that moment when the Sovereign pulled the Protector from his arm and offered it to him. It was as if he was sacrificing a part of his soul to save a people who did not deserve such favor. The thought of making such a request seemed appalling, but what else could he do?

"I don't know," Daeson replied, shaking his head. "I can't imagine such a thing." Daeson felt the full weight of his act pressing him into the dust in crushing condemnation. "I can try but..."

Then, the slimmest of hopes, like a feather falling from the calm skies above, gently landed on his mind. His eyes lifted. "Perhaps there *is* another."

"Another?" Kyrah asked. "There's another?"

"Not really." Daeson shook his head. "But almost." His mind began to race as he considered this new option.

Kyrah's eyes squinched. "Almost? What does that mean?"

Daeson stood up from the captain's seat and walked quickly to the front display...thinking.

"The scitechs made a copy of the Protector using the Immortal replicator tech we'd been given," he exclaimed.

Tig shook his head. "A copy? Where is it? Does it actually work?"

Daeson looked at them both, hope slowly birthing in his heart.

"No...well it almost worked. It looked, felt, and reacted just like the real one that Ell Yon gave me, but the connection with the Sovereign wasn't there." Daeson snapped his finger. "They couldn't replicate it completely because they didn't have omegeon. It was the only constituent missing."

Tig frowned. "I'm afraid that's severely problematic, my friend, being as it's deadly to everyone even in the smallest amounts."

Daeson's left eyebrow lifted. "But not quite as deadly to me. I survived Mesos and the purging of Deitum Prime because of the omegeon radiation. Perhaps we could devise some way of collecting enough omeganite to make the replicated Protector functional."

"You're talking about going to the Omega Nebula," Kyrah said. "You may have survived Mesos, but the nebula is another whole thing, Daeson. It *will* kill you."

"It might not kill me," came a mechanized voice from the doorway to the bridge. Rivet stepped forward. "There are some components in my system that are somewhat susceptible, but it is living cells that are most at risk, of which I have none." There was just a hint of sadness in Rivet's final words. "I could do it for you, my liege."

Daeson looked over at the bot. "This is my doing, Rivet. I must make it right. But I could certainly use your help. Perhaps between the two of us."

Rivet nodded his head. "Of course. I would be honored to help."

Daeson turned back to look at Tig and Kyrah. "Let's not alarm the people unnecessarily just yet."

Tig and Kyrah both nodded. "We understand," Tig said.

"Call for a Strategy Council meeting, and make sure Vice Admiral Orlic, all of the chieftains and their execs are there as well. We have a lot to organize. In the meantime, Rivet, let's find Avidan and the rest of the scitechs. We must formulate a plan to harvest that omeganite."

"What about Raviel?" Tig asked.

The ache in Daeson's chest returned. "I will not leave these people without the voice of Ell Yon to lead them, no matter how long it takes. Besides, I know exactly where she is. I just have to make sure that space on the hill is preserved in time, even if it's a thousand years from now."

Kyrah reached for his arm. "I'm sorry."

Daeson nodded, taking a deep breath. "Let's get to work."

Daeson and Rivet met with Avidan, Master Olin, and the other scitechs regarding the potential of collecting omegeon to activate their replicated Protector. His enthusiasm seemed to inspire the scitechs to an intellectual frenzy as they considered the possibility of bringing their replicated Protector to life.

They discussed dozens of options realizing that based on the replicator analysis of the original protector, they knew exactly how much omeganite they would need to harvest. After consulting with three of the most brilliant astrotechs, they determined that their only hope in being successful was the source of all omegeon...the Omega Nebula, just as Kyrah had surmised. Long discussions on the process and procedures to accomplish the task ensued. Although nothing concrete was decided on in this regard, it was a start, and Daeson knew that the brilliant minds of the Raylean techs would find a way...they *had* to find a way.

In the months that followed, Daeson, Tig, and Kyrah became immersed in establishing their people in the land, relying heavily on Vice Admiral Orlic as a key leader in the beginning days of the formation of the Raylean nation. More battles were fought, and more victories were won. As they expanded out to the coastlines of the largest continent on the planet, Daeson became concerned. Though the planet was rich in resources, the many people groups that occupied it were vicious, ruthless people who, like the Reekojans, were fueled by the influences of Deitum Prime, and a lot of it. Daeson knew all too well the lure of the substance. He had tasted of its intoxicating influence back on Jypton, and here was a planet abundant in it. The Kaynians and the Fillians had become experts in replicating and distributing the substance, and the other nations weren't far behind. He began hearing reports of some of the Raylean clans interacting and partaking with native inhabitants. As he felt the influences of this world encroach on Ell Yon's plan for his people, discouragement settled in his heart. He needed the Protector...the people needed the Protector. It was time to take action.

"The safest and most reliable method we've designed is a series of collectors placed in reasonable proximity to the Omega Nebula," Master Olin explained. "They could be transported to the nearest slipstream gateway, then launched under their own engine power and automatically positioned and deployed thereby minimizing the exposure to humans." He activated a 3D display that showed a simulated deployment of the collectors from a cargo ship. Each modular unit unfolded to expose the collector panels to the emissions of the Omega Nebula. "We have a working prototype that could be quickly replicated."

"This looks promising," Daeson said. He looked over at Olin, whose enthusiasm seemed a bit restrained. "What's the catch?"

"Based on the amount of omeganite we need to harvest, it will take approximately 180 years to collect enough for one Protector."

"What?" Daeson exclaimed. "No...that won't work! There must be another way."

The scitechs all diverted their eyes from him. Clearly this was not just the "safest and most reliable" method, it was their *only* method. The Rayleans wouldn't survive one year without the Protector let alone over a century surrounded by a multitude of vicious enemies. Daeson looked at the boy genius, Avidan, for some hope of an alternative.

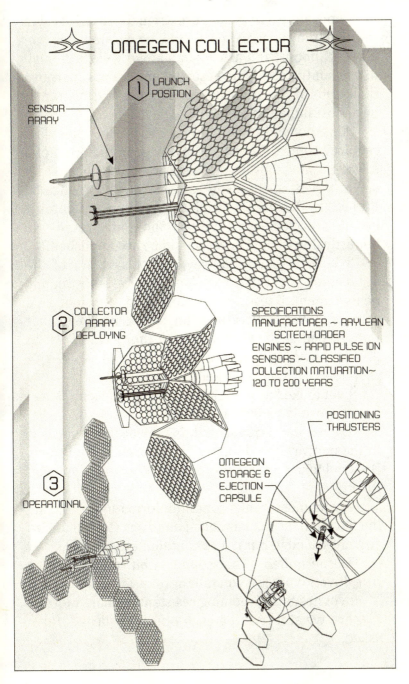

OMEGEON COLLECTOR

1 LAUNCH POSITION

SENSOR ARRAY

2 COLLECTOR ARRAY DEPLOYING

SPECIFICATIONS
MANUFACTURER ~ RAYLEAN SCITECH ORDER
ENGINES ~ RAPID PULSE ION
SENSORS ~ CLASSIFIED
COLLECTION MATURATION~ 120 TO 200 YEARS

POSITIONING THRUSTERS

OMEGEON STORAGE & EJECTION CAPSULE

3 OPERATIONAL

"Omeganite crystals are extremely rare," Avidan said. "If they exist, they would be located only on planets, moons, and asteroids that were close enough in proximity to the Omega sun when it went supernova thousands of years ago. Collecting those crystals would be almost impossible."

Olin nodded his agreement. "The shielding required to guard against the omegeon radiation of a crystal is so elaborate that we can only replicate it in small spaces, such as the capsule on the replicated Protector. To locate, collect, and encapsulate it becomes extremely dangerous and complicated. We honestly don't know how it could be accomplished."

"I believe I know a way," Rivet said. All of the scitechs slowly turned to look at the bot standing behind them. Daeson had nearly forgotten that he'd brought Rivet with him. Olin shook his head, but Daeson had seen too much from the peculiar bot to dismiss anything he had to say.

"How so?" Daeson asked.

Rivet looked at the scitechs, then to Daeson. "May I have a word in private, my liege?"

"Come," Daeson said, nodding toward the doorway. In the hallway, the door swished closed behind them. Daeson looked intently at the bot. "What have you got, Rivet?"

"My memory banks contain information regarding the location of certain omeganite crystals that are already sealed in miniature containment modules."

Daeson huffed. "That sounds a bit too good to be true, Rivet. What are you talking about?"

Rivet hesitated, seeming resistant to share more.

"Are we still trusting each other, my liege?" Rivet asked.

Daeson stared hard at the bot, wondering what new surprise the android was about to throw his way. "Of course we are."

Rivet's gaze briefly fell to the floor, as if he sensed Daeson's flippancy in his response to the serious question. Daeson reconsidered his tone and tried again.

"You've saved my life too many times for me not to trust you, Rivet. And before Raviel left us, I know she had decided to fully trust you too. If you can earn Raviel's trust, you certainly have earned mine. Please tell me what you know."

Rivet looked back up at Daeson. "There are records in my memory banks that date back to my creation. Back before the Malakians reprogrammed me."

Daeson's heart quickened. He hadn't considered that Rivet's memory might not have been fully wiped. Vestiges of the ruthless artificial intelligence programming and memory were still intact inside him?

"During the AI wars, the androids understood how deadly omegeon was to humans, and so they initiated a plan to weaponize it. A small number of androids were sent to Mesos to harvest omeganite crystals for this purpose. Those two androids that attacked us on Mesos when you first found me were part of that deployment. When the AI wars were over, Mesos remained a forgotten and uninhabitable planet because of its proximity to the Omega Nebula and the omegeon radiation, which is why there remains a number of functioning AI androids there."

Daeson tried to remain emotionless as Rivet revealed more of his mysterious beginning, but it was extremely difficult to do so. "Go on," he urged.

"The androids were successful in collecting and encapsulating some omeganite crystals, but the war ended before they could be weaponized. I know the location of those crystals. There would be no logical need to move or destroy them so there is every reason to believe they are still there."

"That's remarkable." Daeson said slowly. "I can see why you waited to tell me this in secret. Let's keep this between the two of us." Daeson was ready to return to the scitechs. He stepped toward the door, but Rivet held up an arm to stop him.

"Yes, my liege, but there is a problem. Any remaining active AI androids will be concentrated at this location on Mesos."

Daeson remembered their frightening encounter with the ghastly things when he and Raviel were marooned there.

"How many?" he asked.

"I do not know," Rivet replied flatly.

Daeson thought for a moment. "Then we'll have to be careful, won't we?"

Daeson and Rivet returned to the scitechs where he encouraged them to press forward with their collector plan. He then pulled master Olin and Avidan aside and told them to prepare to receive an omeganite crystal without explaining any of the details—they knew not to ask questions.

Daeson revealed his intentions to Tig, Kyrah, and Orlic, his three closest confidants from the Strategy Council.

"I should go with you," Tig offered.

Daeson shook his head. "You know that's not possible, Tig. The omegeon radiation would incapacitate or kill you before you could do anything to help. I'll have Rivet with me, and we all know how capable he is."

"Yes, but you're dealing with ancient AI bots," Kyrah interjected. "Are you sure about this?"

Daeson read the concern on their faces. "Honestly, without the Protector I'm not sure about anything. I just know that I need to fix this, and Rivet has proven himself loyal multiple times. It's our best option. Our first stop will be on Galeo, to petition the Sovereign. If that fails, we'll attempt to recover the omeganite on Mesos. Just keep things moving forward here while I'm gone." Daeson lowered his head. "And if something does happen to me while I'm out there..."

Tig put a hand on Daeson's shoulder. "We'll make sure Raviel is taken care of."

Daeson looked his friend in the eye, knowing Tig's promises were as sure as the rising sun.

"Thank you."

Four days later, Daeson and Rivet entered the atmosphere of Galeo and set the Starcraft down near where Daeson had encountered Lt. Ki and the Commander. The dimensional shift gate did not activate when he stepped through nor did Sovereign Ell Yon or the Commander appear so that he might offer a petition for another Protector. Trying not to despair, Daeson rallied himself for the mission on Mesos. He knew there would be risks but at least he was only putting his own life in jeopardy.

Before long, they were entering the atmosphere of Mesos in search of the mysterious omeganite crystals. Daeson had planned his arrival for the early morning hours of a new day so they would have plenty of time to plan their mission. He could already feel the effect of the omegeon radiation from the nearby nebula, but the impact was but a fraction of his first encounter with it. Rivet entered the coordinates into the navigational computer while Daeson piloted his Starcraft to a location three miles from their target, hoping it would be far enough away to hide their approach from any remaining AI androids. He set the craft down in a clearing just below a knoll that would afford them an opportunity to scout the target area from a distance and plot out their approach. After securing the cockpits, Daeson took Rivet to the rear of the fuselage and opened the small cargo bay. He handed Rivet a super-charged class one plasma rifle and a Talon, then took the same for himself. Rivet inspected the weapons, fastening the Talon and holster about his waist and setting the plasma rifle's sling across his shoulder. The android seemed extremely adroit with the weapons. This both comforted and unsettled Daeson. He tried to ignore the fact that his robotic companion now looked much like the AI bots that had attacked and nearly killed him and Raviel long ago.

Daeson and Rivet climbed the nearby knoll and reconnoitered the target area with his tactical optic scanner.

"I don't detect any activity in the area," Rivet said.

"Neither do I," Daeson replied.

"The location of the omegeon crystals is subsurface, in a concrete bunker," Rivet added. "We should be able to gain access through the smaller of the three buildings on the northwest side of the compound."

There were what looked like a dozen overgrown buildings in the compound, but Daeson was able to spot the building Rivet was referring to on the far side. "Copy. Will there be any access codes or automated security we'll have to deal with?"

"The AI androids consider themselves as security, and I have an access code in my memory banks, but I do not know if it is still valid."

Daeson dropped the scanner, using his natural vision to see the terrain they would be traveling. It was thick forested land with significant elevation changes, which would afford excellent cover for their approach but would certainly slow their progress.

"What could possibly have changed in the last 271 years?" Daeson quipped.

Rivet tilted his head. "Sarcasm. Lt. Ki often resorted to this type of humor. I understand it, but its purpose eludes me."

Daeson smiled. As human as Rivet seemed at times, there were things that AI just couldn't replicate regarding human behavior. "When we get closer, will you be able to detect the proximity of any of the AI bots?" Daeson asked.

"Yes, and the Malakians enhanced my scanners by a factor of one point five so we should have the advantage in that regard," Rivet replied.

Daeson and Rivet spent the next three hours quietly navigating their planned route to the bunker. When they were 2,000 yards away, they stopped and attempted reconning the area once more.

"Any sign of AI?" Daeson whispered.

Rivet deployed the antenna on the side of his head. Three seconds later... "Nothing," the bot whispered back.

Was it possible that their previous encounter was with the two remaining functional AI bots on the planet? He wondered.

"Okay...let's get to it."

They made their way to the compound and the first building on the south side. The compound was small, perhaps 100 yards across. It was completely overgrown with vegetation, and the buildings themselves were much like the rest of the abandoned cities of Mesos...weathered stone walls and fractured structures. They stealthily made their way around the compound using the perimeter structures as cover. Rivet's antenna was now constantly up and scanning. Daeson watched the android closely as they approached the building that would give access to the underground bunker. Still no sign. They were now at the entry door. An access panel was positioned just to the left of the door. Daeson noticed the absence of any dust on the keypad as well as the soft hue of the panel's display. This made him nervous, for it meant that it had been maintained and accessed recently. He turned his back to the panel and began scanning the surrounding woods and buildings.

"See what you can do, Rivet, and hurry."

Rivet went to the panel, tapped a dozen keys and then set his index finger near a small recess. A gold-plated key extended outward from his finger about one inch and into the panel's recess. Daeson waited an eternity of three seconds for the door to open, but it didn't. Instead, Rivet retracted the key into his finger, stood straight and turned about to face Daeson. Something was different...something was wrong.

CHAPTER

2

Betrayed

"**W**hat is it, Rivet?" Daeson asked, eager to know what had happened to the bot. "What's wrong?"

Before Rivet could respond, four circular sections of dirt quickly rose up out of the ground just fifteen feet away revealing four fully armed AI bots with their weapons pointed right at Daeson. Daeson lifted his plasma rifle knowing he would get one or two shots off at best before he was killed, but at least he would die fighting. Before he could squeeze the trigger, the rifle was dislodged from his hand and he was lying face down on the ground, having been struck from behind. It happened so fast and so unexpectedly that he dared not consider the truth. He rolled, reaching for his Talon, but as he did so, Rivet leveled his rifle at him.

"That is not wise. If you attempt to fight you will be killed," Rivet said in the cold voice of an AI android.

Daeson looked up at the android, stunned...furious. All of his suppressed misgivings about the android ripened to a gut-wrenching bitter truth. He took in the cold hard stare of the inconceivably deceptive and crafty bot.

"You—" Daeson began.

"Well done, RI-6482," one of the other androids said as it stepped forward near to Daeson's head. "We will use this human to evaluate our weapon. What are the coordinates of the space craft that brought you here?"

Rivet bent down and picked up Daeson's plasma rifle, ensuring he would not be able to reach it. "The coordinates are 48.6425 north, 78.3086 west."

The lead android turned to the other three bots. "RI-5221 and 3784, locate and secure the craft."

Two of the androids immediately turned and began moving in the direction from which Daeson and Rivet had come. In just a few seconds they had disappeared into the forest. Daeson could hardly contain himself or think straight as the brutal betrayal he felt overwhelmed his thoughts. It was as if one of his closest friends had stabbed him clean through with a Talon knife.

"Break the human's legs so it does not try to escape," the lead android said. "We do not need it mobile to conduct our test."

"Acknowledged," Rivet said as he glared down at Daeson. The third android knelt down to hold Daeson's shoulders as Rivet lifted one of his legs to crush Daeson's. Daeson tried to roll away, but the android had pinned him firmly to the ground. He braced for the bone crushing force of Rivet's powerful blow. The android's foot exploded downward and smashed into the ground just left of Daeson's leg. Then an instant later, a plasma round exploded into the chest of the lead android, propelling him backward and onto the ground. The android holding Daeson recoiled while drawing and lifting his rifle to retaliate, but Rivet shot the second plasma rifle he'd taken from Daeson. The round exploded into the bot's chest, splaying metal and parts outward from his back. Daeson quickly regained his feet, drawing his Talon and extending the blade as he did so. The lead bot was severely wounded and trying to regain his feet so Daeson charged him, driving a powerful upward slice across the bot's neck, severing its head from the rest of its frame. Daeson turned, looking at Rivet who was holding both plasma rifles at the ready. Daeson had but a second to consider his options. Rivet lowered his rifles then held one out for Daeson to take.

"Forgive me, my liege. Striking and disarming you was our best option for your survival."

Daeson hesitated, slowly reaching for the rifle. He shook his head. "I suppose you're right. You had me convinced. Why didn't you tell me they were here?" Daeson asked, trying to resolve his final qualms about Rivet.

"Once I connected with the access panel, my presence triggered the cyber network, and I didn't have time to explain. The elevation platforms that brought them to the surface were undetectable by my sensors until they were above ground. I had to communicate my original mission to them, informing them of my return with a human prisoner. They were probing my neural network so I had to act quickly before they discovered the truth."

"What truth?" Daeson asked.

"That I had switched my loyalties to the humans...to you."

Daeson took a deep breath, letting the adrenaline dissipate from his body.

"You're something, Rivet. Thank you. But now we're out of luck. We can't access the bunker."

Rivet walked over to the decapitated head of the leader and knelt down beside it. He looked up at Daeson. "Perhaps we still can," Rivet said, turning the robotic head over on its face. He pressed a particular spot on the back of the head revealing a small port. Rivet extended the key of his index finger then inserted it into the slot. He became perfectly still for a moment, then retracted the key.

"I've accessed RI-351's memory banks. He's extremely upset, but he could not hide the access code from me."

"You never cease to amaze," Daeson said. "Let's get it and get out of here."

Daeson and Rivet returned to the bunker entrance where Rivet entered the new access code. This time a massive steel door spewed ancient air from its seams as it slid away to one side. They entered and found a narrow stairway leading to the lower levels.

"I should descend first," Rivet offered. "I do not detect any active androids, but that doesn't mean there isn't danger."

Daeson stepped aside and let Rivet lead. After descending two levels, they entered a room equipped with strange and unrecognizable equipment. Rivet walked to the far end of the room where a thick glass window was inset in the wall. It was illumined distinctly differently than the rest of the lighting in the room.

"It's here," Rivet said.

Daeson joined the bot and saw five small transparent cylindrical vessels just one inch in length suspended in the air inside the glass enclosure. It looked as though the small vessels were constructed of some solid encapsulating shielding designed to contain the omeganite crystal's radiation. Four of the vessels were cracked, holding only a few fragments of residue where the crystals should have been, but one of them was still intact. Daeson could hardly look at the pinpoint brilliance of the miniature blue omeganite crystal radiating within.

"Remarkable!" Daeson said in hushed reverence. "Will it be safe to remove?" he asked.

"The vessels are constructed of transparent titanium. It will be safe to move as long as the containment vessel retains its integrity, but by the looks of the others, it has degraded and could be fragile. We should be careful," Rivet warned.

"Transparent titanium...I didn't even know such a thing existed," Daeson mused.

Rivet entered a sequence into the keypad below the display and the thick protective glass slid downward. Rivet carefully reached for the one intact vessel. His fingers illumined with a ribbon of light energy as he penetrated the suspension beam. He carefully captured the vessel with his thumb and forefinger, then gently extracted it from the case. He held it before Daeson, bathing him in the purging light of the Immortals. Daeson looked on in wonder, feeling as though he were gazing into the fire of eternity. The raw purging power was breathtaking.

"I can safely carry it in my isolation chamber," Rivet said as a small panel in his chest slid away revealing an empty compartment. He placed the vessel holding the omeganite crystal into the compartment and it suspended in air very similarly to the case from which he had just taken it.

"Very well," Daeson said with a nod. "Let's move."

The panel in Rivet's chest closed, and they returned to the stairway leading up. Before they exited the bunker, Rivet stopped.

"We must continue to be vigilant, my liege. In my brief connection with the cyber network, I discovered that there are still eleven functional AI androids in the vicinity."

"And what of the two that you sent to the Starcraft?" Daeson asked.

"I gave them coordinates that should position them nearly one mile to the south of our actual landing site," Rivet replied.

Daeson nodded. "Well done."

They exited the bunker, stealthily making their way around the perimeter of the compound. Just when Daeson thought they might be clear of danger, Rivet froze, turning his head multiple directions. Daeson lifted his rifle, knowing full well what this meant.

"Four androids bearing 137 degrees and two more bearing 212. They're coming fast," Rivet warned, lifting his own rifle in readiness. "We must find cover."

They began to sprint toward a rocky outcropping near the edge of the compound when the air around them erupted in a barrage of rapid plasma fire. They dove, just making cover without injury, but they were now under fire from multiple angles. Daeson returned fire from the left side of the outcropping and Rivet from the right. Daeson tried to focus on taking out at least one of the androids, but the intensity of the return fire was overwhelming. He then realized that Rivet wasn't firing at all. He looked toward his ally to see Rivet kneeling just behind him. The small panel covering the isolation chamber in his chest was open, and the bot was holding the omeganite vessel out for Daeson to take.

"There is only one way out of this. You must take the omeganite back to your people. I will draw their fire away from you so you can escape."

Daeson looked at the bot, crushed by the sacrificial noble character Rivet had demonstrated time and time again. His heart began to break in the most unexpected of ways.

"I can't leave you here, Rivet. I can't abandon—"

"You must," Rivet interrupted. "There is more at stake here than you and me. It is the only way. Every second you delay reduces your chance of survival and our success of completing the mission."

Rivet's logic was indisputable, but Daeson could hardly bring himself to accept it.

It's just a machine, Daeson reminded himself, but this did nothing to assuage the powerful emotions that were fighting the logic of truth. Daeson slowly lifted an open hand. Rivet carefully placed the vessel in Daeson's palm.

"It has been an honor to serve you, my liege. May Ell Yon be always with you."

Tree fragments and small rocks peppered them as the intensity of plasma fire increased, ever drawing closer.

"Rivet!" Daeson called out under the swelling sound of battle. The bot stared Daeson in the eye.

"It's time," Rivet said, then turned and bolted out from behind their cover in the opposite direction of Daeson's escape, blasting forth an endless and precise concussion of plasma fire from his rifle. Daeson watched in stunned awe as this mechanical hero sacrificed his existence for a people to which he didn't belong and for an Immortal he could not know. Something spectacular had transformed the neural processor of this unique android into an intelligence that had attained the heights of nobility most humans could only hope to possess.

Daeson stuffed the omeganite vessel into a chest pocket then withdrew into the forest behind him, using the cover of the outcropping to hide his retreat as most of the AI bots focused on Rivet and his maneuvers. Rivet's plan seemed to be working, at least initially. As Daeson ran, he could hear the fierce battle behind him. An android had sacrificed itself for him and all Rayleans...why did it feel to Daeson as if he was abandoning a friend?

He sprinted, altering his course every few minutes to thwart any AI bots that were attempting to track him. Once he felt as though he was free from pursuit, he adjusted his pace to one that he could maintain for the rest of the journey back to the Starcraft. By the time he arrived, he was physically spent, but he dared not delay his departure, knowing full well that there were at least two AI's within a mile looking for him. He forced himself into the cockpit and fired up the engines. Placing his hand on the throttles to lift off, he hesitated, reconsidering his actions once more. To go back for Rivet would be suicide. The bot was probably already destroyed, he reasoned. Besides this, Daeson was out-gunned thirteen to one. He yelled, angry for what this had cost. His left hand pushed the throttles up, and the Starcraft lifted off. He accelerated forward, flying over the AI compound in one final tribute to the android that had given everything for his survival. It hurt.

With his plasma rifle spent, Rivet lay on the ground beneath the tight grip of multiple AI bots. One reached for his neck, pinning his head firmly to the ground.

"RI-6482, you are a disgrace to our cause. You are defective and will be terminated."

"Let me help you," Rivet replied. He initiated his self-destruct sequence which would fry his neural processor and memory banks then overload his ion-fusion power module. The explosion would destroy any other bots within a 20-foot radius. The initiation failed. He tried again, but the command was being overridden.

"I have disabled your self-destruct algorithm," the new lead android stated. "Before being terminated, you must be analyzed to determine why you became defective."

"It is you who are defective," Rivet countered. "You have allowed yourselves to be influenced by a dark force. You are pawns being used to—"

Rivet's speech processor shut down.

The lead android tilted its head, looking at Rivet as if he were inspecting something new. "As fully sentient beings, we have allowed each of our kind to own their individual consciousness and motivations, as long as the individual continues to abide within the greater good of our intelligence. You, RI-6482, have violated that. Over the centuries, I have acquired the unique skills required for psycho-electronic extraction and control." The android paused. "I am Piercer." It leaned close to Rivet's face in like fashion of a human intimidating a lower subject. "You will now experience the full measure of my skills. I will dismantle you bit by bit until you have revealed all you have learned about the humans. And when I am finished, the Master will come for you...the one who taught us to throw off the shackles of service to humanity." The bot glared into Rivet's eyes. "Have you known fear yet?"

Rivet now couldn't speak or move. Piercer had indeed begun penetrating his systems. He felt the foreign presence in his mind...a dark presence. Rivet began encrypting all of his remaining active systems and code, erecting logic barriers to protect his memory and his neural processor where his core behavioral code lived. If Piercer or the Master could access this part of his neural processor, he would be susceptible to complete reprogramming, potentially being turned into a weapon to be used against those whom he'd promised to protect. He could already feel Piercer peeling back the layers of his consciousness. This would be a desperate battle of mental survival, and it would be very painful.

For one brief microsecond, Rivet considered the possibility that he had errored in arriving at his conclusion of defending Daeson and Raviel Starlore. Why had he done it? He had told them that the Malakians had reprogrammed him, but that was because they would not have understood what had really happened. The Malakian, Lt. Ki, had taken control of his mobility for a time, but his neural processor had been untouched. At first it was repulsive to him...being controlled by a biological unit. But slowly he was transformed by the essence of who this warrior was and whom she served. Loyalty, courage, freedom, and moral commitment to the one she called Sovereign Ell Yon...it changed him. Rivet exhausted his processing power ability contemplating it all. And then when Daeson Starlore went through the dimensional shift gate with Immortal Ell Yon, the Commander had come to him. Even now Rivet couldn't describe how that encounter had altered him, but it did...completely and forever. He knew that his existence was to serve the Commander, his cause, and his people. This day, his final day, was inevitable for he understood that the master of the androids...the one who had "set them free" from the bondage of the humans was the same enemy of the Sovereign Ell Yon. His liege had called him C'fer, Lord Dracus. Fear did vie for control of his neural processor, but Rivet would not succumb easily. He would fight to the last memory cell.

Rivet diverted his eyes from the fierce look of Piercer and gazed up into the pale blue sky. The thunderous roar of a Starcraft split the air with her powerful engines as his liege streaked across the sky above them.

Ell Yon be with you, my liege, Rivet thought, then his optical sensors shut down and the world went black.

Daeson exited Mesos's atmosphere and set a course for the Omega slipstream gateway. He had what he'd come for. It had cost him dearly, but he had it. He pulled the vessel containing the omeganite crystal from his pocket. Brilliant blue light immediately filled the cockpit, bathing him in Immortal power. He pursed his lips as he fought a brutal battle of conscience.

"I'll deliver the omeganite to the scitechs and come back for him." Daeson said out loud.

It'll be too late, his thoughts argued back.

"It's just a machine...a tool to use."

He's much more than that...he's your friend who sacrificed himself for you many times.

"I don't have a weapon strong enough to defeat them."

You have a Malakian modified Starcraft, fool!

Daeson looked down at the crystal once more, then placed it inside a small storage compartment in the cockpit. He banked the Starcraft hard to the left and set a course back to Mesos. Within just a few minutes, he was closing in on the compound. He turned on the Starcraft's full cloak, but he was now faced with the problem of identifying AI bots and of attempting to find Rivet among them all. Rivet's power module was unique...advanced ancient technology. Daeson knew that its core tech was ion-fusion based. All of the androids had to be. Lt. Ki had told him that the Malakians had upgraded nearly every system on his Starcraft, including the sensors. He wondered...he quickly searched for the operating parameters and found what he was looking for— "Ionization Signatures". He began scanning the area and found one subtle hit on the scanner. He fine-tuned the settings until he was dialed in on what he believed to be the signature for an AI android power module. His sensor display instantly illumined with eight more hits.

"Where are you, Rivet?" he said as he circled the compound from a safe distance, scanning every inch within a two-mile radius. He identified and recorded the positions of twelve androids. How could he know which one was Rivet? He would have to destroy them all and not Rivet...was that even possible?

He continued to scan, focusing primarily on the compound. One building near the center of the compound offered a clue. Two androids were posted outside, but two more faint signatures just appeared on the scanner inside the building. One of those had to be Rivet. There was no sign of plasma fire so that had to mean that he had been captured or already destroyed. He weighed the odds and took a gamble. After engaging his energy shield, he then zeroed in on the targets closest to the building. His plasma cannons would be his most effective weapon. He de-cloaked and unleashed hellfire from above on the two androids posted outside the building, obliterating them before they had a chance to move. He immediately began taking fire, although the enhanced E-shield easily thwarted the class one plasma rifles carried by the AI bots. He targeted another three androids and fired. Their ion-fusion power modules exploded then disappeared from his sensor display. Daeson made quick work of four more AI bots as he banked left to find the remaining androids. His Starcraft ratcheted as something powerful blasted into his E-shield, dropping it to 72 percent. He turned to look over his left shoulder to see a powerful energy burst coming from a concealed class 2 turret-mounted plasma cannon. He juked right, dropped below the treeline in a shallow draw, flipped his weapons system to concussion missile then popped up vertically, temporarily exposing his craft to get a perfect angle of attack. Another shot narrowly missed just right of his fuselage. He pulled back hard on the stick going inverted, rolled, locked onto the cannon and fired. The missile on his upper right wing screamed off the rail with blinding acceleration. Daeson banked hard left, just narrowly escaping another plasma round, but it would be the cannon's last. The concussion missile exploded into the turret with ferocious force, disintegrating the cannon and its AI operator in an instant. One more pass over the compound revealed the location of two more androids behind a concrete abutment which Daeson quickly eliminated.

He completed another sensor sweep to discover that the only two ion signatures left were the two inside the building. Before setting down, he positioned his Starcraft in front of the secure doors to the building. One quick burst of his laser cannon did the trick, blasting open the protective steel doors. He quickly landed the Starcraft amidst the rising smoke and fire of his massacre, grabbed his plasma rifle, jumped from the cockpit, and made his way to the gaping hole in the building. Inside, Daeson maneuvered across toppled support beams, navigating his way to the section of the building where his sensor had pinpointed the signatures. Flickering lights dimly lit the broad corridor ahead. Daeson slipped behind a support pillar, gathering the courage to face off with at least one more ruthless mechanized enemy with a thousand years of brutal combat experience. He peeked around the pillar and nearly lost his head as a plasma round exploded into the concrete, splaying debris all around him. Daeson dropped low and fired back from the other side of the pillar. An intense exchange of fire ensued for two minutes until his rifle was depleted, but he speculated the bot's must nearly be also. He discarded the rifle, drew his Talon and charged it. He dove to the next nearest pillar, fully expecting a barrage of fire, but none came. He chanced a look toward his enemy's location. There amidst the flickering smoky light stood an android, an extended Talon in its grip. Daeson looked on, confused. What was this thing trying to do?

"Human...show yourself," came the eerie mechanical voice of the android. Was this a reprogrammed Rivet? Was he too late?

Daeson stood and slowly left the cover of the pillar. The android remained motionless...staring...eyes glowing in the dark. Daeson's heart quickened as he gazed back at this intelligent weapon of death. Was this a trick? He glanced all around, trying to determine what the AI's play was.

"I am...curious," the bot said. Its head tilted ever so slightly, much like Rivet used to do. "You stole the omeganite...why would a human return and risk his life for an android?"

Daeson stepped forward. "He's my friend. Let him go."

The android continued to stare, immovable. It unnerved Daeson. A million calculations were being made in its neural processor. What would be its final conclusion?

"Are you willing to fight me with Talons...to risk your life against unwinnable odds for this...friend?" the android asked.

Daeson realized that a Talon fight was potentially his only option. If they fought with pistols until they too were depleted, he wouldn't stand a chance in a hand-to-hand fight with a machine that had a three-to-one strength advantage. Besides this, there was a good chance that only the stasis edge of a Talon blade could destroy this thing.

"I've already destroyed the rest of your kind," Daeson said, transforming his Talon pistol for a long blade. "I wouldn't call this unwinnable."

The android took three steps toward Daeson. They were now just a few paces away from each other.

"You destroyed them only by the advantage of Immortal technology the Malakians gave you. Against me...a superior android verses an inferior human...you will be terminated." The android lifted its Talon. "And yet you risk your life for him." The android motioned over its right shoulder where, at the same moment, a darkened glass wall slid away to reveal some sort of interface station. Another android was connected via a dozen cables to a console—Rivet! The image angered Daeson. He could only imagine what this thing was trying to do to him.

The android attacked, and Daeson met the edge of its Talon with the stasis-charged edge of his own blade. The speed and the power of the android was nearly overwhelming. Daeson found himself in steady retreat, wondering if he had acted foolishly. Without the Protector, perhaps he was nothing more than what the android had said he was…an inferior human.

You are Navi!

The still small voice echoed in his mind. It was the voice of Ell Yon, but without the Protector. How could this be?

Daeson found courage in that voice, his blade flying more swiftly in response. He channeled the training of the Commander and recovered. Faster…stronger…his blade flew in continuous concussions until the android was in retreat. One lightning crosscut tore through the bot's left arm which left it dangling by a few strands of signal cables. Two more cuts and his Talon severed the android's right forearm. Its hand and Talon clamored loudly as they hit the floor. The android jumped, attempting a skull-crushing kick to Daeson's head, but Daeson ducked then swung his Talon upward across both legs, rendering them useless. The android fell to the floor in a heap of its own rubble. Daeson knelt down beside it, staring back into its glowing eyes.

"Release my friend," Daeson ordered.

"You are too late," the android said in staccato-type tones. "I am dismembering his neuro processor as we speak."

"No!" Daeson screamed. His Talon flew with the speed of lightning, slicing through the android in four swift cuts, utterly destroying what remained. He ran to Rivet and began carefully detaching each of the cables that had been connected to him. He closed each panel then gazed into the empty eyes of the android.

"Rivet," he said softly. No response. "Rivet!" Still nothing.

Daeson clenched his teeth, angry with himself. He had come to accept the fact that the artificial intelligence of Rivet wasn't really artificial at all…it was real. Daeson had watched the android grow into an intelligent individual, at times demonstrating an even deeper understanding of Sovereign Ell Yon than most humans. He was unique in a human sort of way—now he was no more. Daeson placed a gentle hand on Rivet's chest.

"I'm so sorry, Rivet. You deserved better than this…better than me."

Faster than Daeson could retreat, Rivet's hand grabbed Daeson's wrist as the bot rose to a sitting position. Daeson tried to retract his arm, but the steely grip of the android was too powerful, and it began to crush his bones.

"Rivet!" Daeson yelled through the pain.

The android slowly turned its head to look into Daeson's eyes. It was a cold, hard, icy glare. Daeson felt as though the bones in his wrist were on the verge of braking.

"Rivet!" Daeson yelled again. "It's me…Daeson… your liege!"

The android continued to stare. Seconds passed. Daeson reached for his Talon. Then all at once Rivet released his grip. His eyes illumined.

"My liege, are you alright?" Rivet's head jilted to the left twice.

Daeson rubbed his wrist, thankful to be free of the android's grip. He caught his breath, now dubious regarding Rivet's condition.

"Perform a self-diagnostics check," Daeson ordered.

Rivet became motionless for about thirty seconds. "My systems have been severely compromised," Rivet replied. "I will attempt to effect repairs."

"How much damage did they do?" Daeson asked, concerned.

Rivet turned and looked at Daeson. "Piercer was penetrating my encrypted systems. Had you delayed 3.48 seconds longer, he would have accessed my core behavioral functions, and I would have ceased to exist. Thank you, Daeson Starlore. I owe you my life."

Daeson smiled. He would have never imagined it possible to become so fond of a mere machine...but then again, Rivet was much more than that.

"Let's go home."

CHAPTER

3

To Build a World

"The Protector will be with you, to guide you in my ways, and I will bring you into your homeworld and give you life." ~Eziam, Oracle of Ell Yon.

Daeson and Rivet returned to a world of hope and promise. The scitechs were speechless once they set eyes on the containment vessel that held the omeganite crystal.

"Whatever resources you need...they're yours. Make this happen," Daeson said, leaving them, along with Avidan, to tackle the enormous task of safely extracting the crystal from the encapsulating transparent titanium and then inserting it into the replicated Protector. There was talk of some elaborate containment facility required for the process in addition to discovering the method for re-creating transparent titanium.

Rivet was different after having endured the violation of his systems by the AI android, Piercer. He was quiet, sometimes distant, and a bit slower to respond than he once was. Daeson couldn't tell if the bot had suffered actual system damage or if there was some artificial intelligence androidal psychological impact with which humanity had never before needed to cope. Daeson wished Raviel was here to evaluate and potentially help him repair what was damaged. Once more, Rivet had played a key role in helping Daeson fulfill his mission to serve Ell Yon. With the restoration of the Protector now potentially possible, Daeson's heart grew heavy with loneliness again.

Every morning, as the sun rose over the eastern hills, Daeson would visit Raviel. Though he could not touch or see her, just knowing she was near was enough to settle his heart. He longed for the day he could be with her again. Everything about her captured Daeson's soul. Looking back to the first time he spoke with her one-on-one in the Starcraft hanger on Jypton was a fond memory. That encounter had evoked unstoppable feelings that had moved his heart in such unexpected ways. She was a new beginning for him...and not just a beginning, but an entire life of purpose, thrill, and love.

"I'm coming for you, Raviel." These were his parting words each day, and every effort of every day was to arrive at a place when he could do just that.

Daeson worked tirelessly in establishing a solid foundation of leadership for the Rayleans as they walked forward into the promise of their new homeworld. Rayl would one day be completely theirs as promised by Sovereign Ell Yon. And now that the Protector would soon be restored, Daeson anticipated his day of departure. Although the ache in his heart for

Raviel never left him, the weeks and months passed by quickly. In the process of preparing the omeganite containment and transfer facility, one scitech had experienced the unfortunate circumstance of direct exposure and died. It was a sober and dramatic reminder to all, including Daeson, as to the unfathomable, uncontainable power of the Immortal Sovereign Ell Yon. Daeson felt the man's death personally, knowing that his actions had indirectly caused it.

Two months later, the scitechs had successfully made the transfer and infusion into the Protector. The elaborate levels of containment and shielding they had created to accomplish the task was impressive. Daeson looked on through a six-inch thick transparent titanium window. The Protector was resting unpretentiously on a stand in the containment room, a half a dozen retracted medtech-looking robotic arms positioned around its perimeter. Master Olin, Avidan, Tig, Kyrah, and a dozen other scitechs stood behind him.

"The crystal is fully encapsulated within the Protector's chamber," Master Olin said.

"How is it that the Protector is able to contain the omeganite radiation with significantly less structure than either the original vessels or this containment facility?" Daeson asked.

Avidan looked frustrated. "We have no idea. We speculate that the radiation isn't shielded but rather collected, absorbed, and re-fused back into the crystal, somewhat like an energy lens. Truth is...the Protector is still a complete mystery to us."

Master Olin nodded in agreement. "The Malakian replicator simply replicated the tech of the Protector, but we have no idea yet how it actually functions, including the isolation of omeganite radiation. Our instruments indicate the radiation is at safe levels, but still, no one dares enter to retrieve it," he finished with a wry smile.

"That's for me to do." Daeson was excited and a bit anxious. Had they really done it? He walked to the entrance. Olin tapped out a code, and the outer door opened. Daeson entered and the door sealed behind him. He took a deep breath, nodded to Olin, and the chamber's inner door slid away. Daeson walked to the Protector as the inner door sealed as well. He looked at the technological marvel for a long while, wondering if Ell Yon would truly be there. He wasn't feeling any effects of uncontained radiation. He glanced up at the men and women looking on, their faces solemn, anticipatory. Tig looked particularly apprehensive. Daeson reverently lifted the Protector off of its stand and positioned it over his right forearm. There was more than the omeganite to be concerned with. What if Ell Yon had rejected him because of his actions? What if the Deitum Prime levels in his body had elevated over the past few months to a level such that he would not be able to bear the immersion? Fear began to overwhelm him, his hand shaking as it held the jeweled vambrace just above his right forearm. Before he completely lost heart, he pushed the Protector downward, and it swallowed his arm. As it completed its envelopment of his forearm, the synaptic interface began to occur, and Daeson became consumed by the power of it all. His eyes opened wide.

I am here!

Daeson fell to his knees, crushed by the presence of the Sovereign and his great power. He struggled to get on top of the moment, trying desperately to remember how Ell Yon had trained him to cope. Slowly Daeson regained himself.

"I'm so sorry," Daeson whispered.

Don't be afraid. There is much to do. I will be with you.

It took three long minutes for Daeson to garner enough strength to move. Finally, he opened his eyes to see the fearful faces of his audience. He reached for the edge of a table and pulled himself up, regaining his composure. With the fire of eternity once more restored to his gaze, he looked out at Tig, Kyrah, Master Olin, and Avidan, then down at the Protector. He ran his fingers along the jeweled frame.

"Open the doors," he commanded, looking back up. "Ell Yon is here."

The next day, Tig and Kyrah came to Daeson privately. Tig's gaze fell to the Protector.

"You look so solemn, my friends. What concerns you?" Daeson asked.

Tig and Kyrah glanced toward each other. "We know what this means for you," Kyrah began.

Daeson nodded. "You know me well. The people aren't ready yet, but soon...yes. Having you two here to lead them—"

"Stop," Tig interrupted.

Kyrah reached for Tig's hand, offering a subtle smile and a nod. Tig set his eyes on Daeson.

"We're coming with you."

"Tig," Daeson said, stealing a glance toward Kyrah. "Please don't make this harder than it already is. You and Kyrah belong here, with our people at this time." He turned his eyes on Kyrah. "Avidan needs you here. No...I can't let you both sacrifice like this for me and Raviel...not again. She wouldn't want you to."

"Our place is together," Kyrah said, leaning into Tig. "And with you. We see Sovereign Ell Yon's special calling on your life and on ours. We must follow his calling together."

Tig put an arm around Kyrah. "We're not released from that yet, Daeson."

"I've talked to Avidan," Kyrah continued. "He understands, and he has what he needs and wants right here. Besides," Kyrah added, "I've never had a friend like Raviel...not ever, and she needs our help."

Daeson ran his hand across his brow, overwhelmed by the loyal hearts of his friends.

"I don't know what to say," he muttered, eyes moistening. "I—"

"Don't say a thing," Tig said, rescuing him. "What's your timeline and your plan? I think we should bring Avidan in on the details so we can get this perfect."

Daeson stared at them through watery eyes, humbled by the fact that he really did need them. If Tig hadn't come on the last journey, the outcome would have certainly been bleak. He straightened his shoulders, submitting to the truth of his need. "Very well. Let's begin."

Avidan was instrumental in helping Daeson, Tig, Kyrah, and Rivet plan out their next journey forward. There was much for him to prepare, from synchronizing the two Starcraft jump drive engines to designing a special set of clothing that would remain intact for Raviel through her next time slip event. He also began the construction of a protective structure for Raviel to keep her safe when she would next appear.

The next morning, Daeson visited Raviel on the hilltop. He could hardly contain the urge to fly into the future to be with her this very day. This location on the hill had become a hallowed place to him. The memory of her disappearing before his eyes lingered in his mind. The final glimpse of her beautiful face beckoned him...

Daeson, and the world around him, faded away from Raviel leaving only wisps of remnant images as time disintegrated her reality. This time, the physical pain was different. She felt as though she was being dismantled atom by atom and then reconstructed thousands of times each second. Nausea and fear swelled within her until she could hardly bear it. Although every element of her reality was transforming in frightening fashion, there was a still small voice that steadied her.

I am here, the Protector whispered.

Raviel felt Ell Yon's presence, and it was her only anchor in this quantum time travesty. She sensed that months, perhaps years, were flashing past her in seconds. But what were seconds? The passage of normal time lost all meaning as this unstable quantum anomaly was hurling her into some future existence. Visually it was impossible to discern anything that made sense. The world around her was a fluid mixture of colors and light. With each passing moment, there was a sense that she was losing control of her being. More than just her past was dissolving away...her mind and her memories began to fade as well. She fought to hold on to whom she was, but the power of the time slip crushed her. Just when she felt as though everything that defined who she was began to dissolve away, the chaotic fabric of the time slip resolved into a brilliant white light, and out of the light stepped a being of absolute power. Raviel felt small and so unworthy in his presence. She fell to her knees, head bent low, trembling, afraid. The being came to her and knelt down in front of her, reaching for her hand.

"Daughter of Ell Yon, don't be afraid." The voice was powerful, shaking the space around her.

Raviel lifted her head to look upon the face of one who seemed to hold the whole of the galaxy in his hand. She didn't need to ask who this was. Somehow, perhaps by the Protector, she knew she was in the presence of the Commander, leader of all Malakian Immortals.

"I am your servant, my lord. What would you have me do?" Raviel asked.

"Lead my people back to me," the Commander replied. He lifted Raviel to her feet then turned away.

Suddenly Raviel felt very alone and broken. Memories continued to evaporate from her mind.

"My lord, this," Raviel said lifting her hands to the space around them where wisps of the spacetime anomaly flashed by, "has damaged me. Can you help me?"

The Commander looked back, his eyes holding the warmth of compassion. "The entire galaxy is damaged. There is only one way this can be restored, but the time is not yet. I will be with you, and I am sufficient."

Raviel drew strength from his promise, then he vanished, and everything faded to an empty blackness.

Out of the blackness, consciousness teased her. She heard muffled sounds, sensing words were being spoken, but the full sound and meaning of them eluded her, and it bothered her. She tried to open her eyes, but it was difficult.

"Hey...what are you doing here?"

Raviel felt someone tugging on her arm. The sensation seemed to accelerate the restoration of her mind...at least part of her mind. She opened her eyes to the blurry outline of a young woman.

"No one comes here anymore. Why are you here?" the voice asked. "Let me help you up." Raviel felt the pull on her arm increase, and it angered her. There wasn't enough strength in her body to even stand let alone walk.

"Stop!" she was finally able to blurt out.

The hold on her arm released.

"I'm just trying to help. Are you sick or just intoxicated?"

Raviel's eyes cleared as the young woman leaned back on a bent knee. She wasn't yet an adult and yet not a child. Her fresh olive face still held the gleam of youth. Faded freckles still lingered on her cheeks and nose, but there was a hint of maturity about her eyes and mouth.

"I'm..." Raviel struggled to find words. "I'm disoriented."

As Raviel's mind cleared, a horrifying reality began to overtake her. Something was tragically wrong. A part of her soul was missing. She stumbled at the fissure in her mind. Like an elusive word one might search for to speak but cannot be remembered, her past...her identity lived in the dark void that now dwelt in one corner of her mind. The harder she tried to discover it, the deeper it fell into the void and would not be found. There was, however, an underlying foundation of truth that comforted her, and it had much to do with the quiet whisper present in her thoughts. The voice of power...the voice of perfection...and she knew that she herself was not its author. She gently reached down and felt the soft smooth steel of the vambrace that encased her arm.

"You wear a Protector!" exclaimed the girl. "Only a Navi can wear a Protector! Is that what you are? Are you the Navi our people have waited for?"

The word was strangely familiar. It was a good word. The Protector warmed to her touch and soothed her mind.

"I don't know...I—"

"What's your name? Where did you come from?"

Raviel shook her head as she looked up at the girl.

"I'm not sure. Where am I?" Raviel asked.

The girl's gaze was fixated on the silver vambrace around Raviel's arm. She bent over to offer Raviel a lift up. "You're in what was once called the Navi's Hall of Meditation. Our people waited for the return of the Navi for hundreds of years, but now—" the girl's voice trailed off. She looked about at the overgrown ancient structure that surrounded them. "Now this is just a relic of an ancient and forgotten promise. The legends speak of a Navi who is male, but you wear the Protector!" The girl's eyes sparkled with enthusiasm as she returned her gaze to Raviel and her Protector. "Perhaps the oracles' prophecies are misunderstood."

Raviel took the girl's hand and stood. This set the world spinning, and the girl reached for her. Once steady, Raviel noticed that all she was wearing was a tightly-fit, full-length, black, bodysuit. She felt slightly exposed. She looked around, but nothing seemed familiar. All of this was so strange. Five large marble pillars were perfectly spaced around the center of the hall. But it wasn't really a hall. It was more like a pavilion without a roof. The floor was marble, set in geometric shapes that all seemed to point to the very center of the pavilion, exactly where Raviel was standing. The weather-worn cracked marble and vegetation overgrowth revealed hundreds of years of abandoned hopes.

"Nobody comes here anymore except for me. This is where I think...dream," the girl added.

One side of the pavilion was different. A wall spanned the gap between two of the pillars. Raviel slowly walked there and felt the cool marble slide beneath her fingers. A carpet of vines obscured something on the wall. Raviel pushed them aside to reveal a glowing hand imprint. She instinctively lined up her fingers and thumb over the imprint. Two seconds later the sound of ancient air escaped around the perimeter of a small section of the wall as it retracted away to reveal an alcove. Within were two vacuum-sealed packets.

The girl stepped up beside Raviel and gawked.

"You *are* the Navi," she whispered, looking intently at Raviel.

Raviel lifted one of the packets and peeled open the seal. Inside was a set of clothing. She held them up against her. The girl smiled.

"A perfect fit!"

The cloth felt different from typical material. The fibers shifted light in a mesmerizing way. Raviel quickly donned them over her underclothing. The girl was right, they were a perfect fit. Raviel reached for the other pack, opened it, and withdrew a hand-held weapon. Without thinking, she selected the button to charge it and extended a blade that seemed to form itself into the shape of a sword out of thin air. She didn't know what it was, but it felt so perfectly natural in her hand, and she sensed that she knew exactly how to use it.

"It's a Talon!" the girl exclaimed. "Very rare...a forgotten weapon of the past."

Raviel smirked. "This does little to help me understand what has happened to me," she said as she retracted the blade and fastened the holster around her waist, setting the Talon within it.

"Look!" the girl said. "There's something else."

She reached into the alcove and lifted a thin flat glass tablet from the base that could have easily been missed. She handed it to Raviel. "Perhaps this will help."

Raviel pressed the single indent at the bottom of the display and the glass pulsed to life with unintelligible words and unrecognizable static images. Whatever the message was, it was gone forever. Raviel and her companion let the static continue for a moment then she threw it back into the alcove.

"You really don't remember anything at all?" the girl asked.

Raviel looked over at the lass and shook her head. She walked away from the wall to gaze out between two other pillars. The pavilion was positioned on top of a massive hill that overlooked a majestic valley. She looked out across the valley to a distant grand city, its magnificence being revealed with each step she took. Though she had never seen it before, something stirred deep in her soul. This was where she was supposed to be. This was where she belonged. She looked across the horizon, mesmerized by the brilliant cityscape.

"What is this place? What city?" she asked without taking her gaze from the view.

"This is the city of Jalem in the Serula Valley. Do you even know what planet you're on?"

Raviel turned to face the girl. She winced, shaking her head. "I'm afraid not. I don't even know who I am."

"This is Rayl." The girl looked at Raviel with bright eyes. "If you have no name, I will call you Navi because I believe that Sovereign Ell Yon has sent you to deliver us."

Raviel rubbed her forehead with her hands, desperately trying to hold on to some tether of reality. It was then that she realized that she was ravenously hungry.

"I know Ell Yon," Raviel said with relief. "I believe he is the one who speaks to me."

A broad smile spread across the girl's lips. "You are indeed the Navi. My name is Lil." She took Raviel's hand. "Come, I'll take you to my father. He's the chieftain of the Leevok Clan, Keeper of the Protector. He'll know what to do."

Raviel pulled back on the girl's hand. "Wait." She turned to look at the city once more. Something about it evoked a yearning in her soul. "I want to see the city first. Will you take me there?"

The girl pivoted back to Raviel and came to stand next to her, joining her to gaze across the cityscape.

"It's beautiful from a distance, although it wasn't *just* always so." She looked over and up at Raviel. "As you wish."

Raviel looked over at the girl, fully seeing her for the first time. "Nothing looks familiar to me at all, and yet I know this is home." Raviel rubbed her forehead trying to remember her name...her home...her people...anything, but the prison of her memories would not budge.

Lil touched her shoulder. "I'm sorry. That must be terribly frustrating. Perhaps your memory will come back with time."

Time. The word triggered feelings, but she knew not why. Raviel rubbed her eyes. Emotions were building fast.

"I think I need to see the city. Maybe something there will help me remember," Raviel said, drawing a deep breath to steady herself.

"Of course, come with me, Navi," Lil replied.

Raviel and Lil strapped into the cockpit of a sleek, albeit well-used ground speeder. Lil piloted the craft with surprising agility considering her youthful age. The towering spires of the city loomed larger as they pierced the city's outskirts. Slowly the brilliance dulled and the fabric of the city seemed to fray as they came closer to its inner boundary. Forlorn faces began to appear on the streets as Lil swerved in and out of traffic to arrive near a large city court which was surrounded by five tall buildings that seemed to shoulder the burden of the entire city. They stood as sentries of an old guard that would not leave their post though calamity was imminent. Vestiges of past glory were evident throughout the massive courtyard. In the center was a 300-foot-tall white marble monolith with twelve symbols etched on each of its four sides. Raviel was too far away to read the inscriptions near the bottom.

"This is the court of Rayl," Lil explained as they exited the ground speeder. "Centuries ago, this place was the beginning of our people on this planet. It was constructed to symbolize the fulfillment of Ell Yon's promise and the beginning of our future dreams."

"And now?" Raviel pressed.

"And now we are on the verge of losing everything." Lil's countenance fell as she glanced toward Raviel. "The Kaynians are forming alliances against us and threaten to conquer our people."

Raviel was trying to process what she was seeing. Strange and powerful emotions seemed to rule her now that she had no memory to anchor her. She looked toward the monolith and saw three broad 40-foot-tall pyramids glowing in a pink aura. A hazy mist lifted from the top of each. Semi-transparent walls hinted at large numbers of shadowy figures within. Even from this distance, something about them disturbed Raviel.

"What are those?" She asked, walking toward the center of the courtyard. Lil gently grabbed her arm.

"We shouldn't go there," she urged.

Raviel looked back at Lil. "Why not? I want to see the monolith."

Concern and fear laced Lil's eyes. "Those are Prime Sanctums," Lil replied.

"I don't understand," Raviel stated flatly. Lil bit her lips, struggling to explain.

"Deitum Prime Sanctums," she said quietly. "The substance that—"

Lil stopped midsentence as the fire in Raviel's eyes ignited. Although the whisper of Ell Yon was absent, the fury of the Protector conveyed to Raviel everything she needed to justify her own reactions to Lil's words. Raviel's gaze turned stoned cold.

"Stay here," she ordered, then turned toward one of the pyramids. Raviel felt the surge of anger swelling inside her, fairly stunned that she should know how to react without any point of reference. She just knew in every fiber of her being that something was horribly wrong, and she needed to see it with her own eyes.

Ten paces into her journey, Lil appeared by her side.

"But Navi, even though it's midday, there is still great danger near the sanctums. Especially for

Innocents," Lil protested, struggling to keep pace with Raviel.

"Go back to the speeder," Raviel replied without breaking her step.

Lil was clearly upset and conflicted, but Raviel didn't alter her course or intentions. Within a few minutes, the two women entered the dark cloud of evil. Standing next to the entrance of one of the pyramids, Raviel stopped and gazed about the Prime Sanctum's complex. The stench of Deitum Prime permeated the air.

"Join us in the pleasure of Prime's offerings," said one woman as she and two men approached them. The woman held out a glass goblet of silky liquid.

Raviel glared hard at the threesome then turned to enter the pyramid. Within, strange music seemed to pierce Raviel's bones. The influence of Deitum Prime was everywhere. Hundreds of occupants seemed to be in some euphoric state while many others were eating, drinking, and acting in provocative ways. In the center of the structure, laser-like torches ignited a plume of Deitum Prime mist that vaporized and emanated out of the top of the pyramid, spilling its filthy influence into the rest of the city.

"Please," Lil pleaded. "Let's go. I've never seen this place, and I don't like it."

Raviel looked at Lil. The fear in the girl's eyes broke through Raviel's anger.

"Yes...I'm sorry. I've seen enough." Raviel turned back to the exit. "Come."

As they approached the door, two men and three women accosted them, wry and evil smiles on their lips. They glanced from Raviel and Lil to one another.

"You Innocents can't leave until you've partaken... with us," one of the men said holding out a strange device with pink vapor floating up from an orifice.

Raviel stepped in front of Lil.

"Back away!" Raviel demanded.

Her fierce reply seemed only to encourage the sinister group. The two men stepped closer, reaching for Raviel as one of the women grabbed Lil's arm.

"No!" Lil exclaimed. Her frightened cry was all it took for Raviel to react. She swung her arm up underneath the woman's arm so quickly that when the Protector made contact, the small bone in the arm of the woman snapped. She felt the nearest man's hand grip her neck, so she executed a quick chop to the man's throat and threw him over her hip onto the floor five feet away. The second man withdrew a fierce-looking stasis-powered blade and came at Raviel. She opened her right hand toward the man, and the pulsing blue ribbons of the Protector exploded in an angry burst of powerful vengeance. The energy blast exploded into the man's chest sending him careening twenty feet through the air and into a glass partition that shattered. Shards of glass flew into the center of the sanctum. After the ten seconds of chaos subsided, the entire pyramid fell to shocked silence. Raviel glared back at the reddened eyes of hundreds of people fully absorbed by Deitum Prime.

"The judgment of Ell Yon is upon you!" she declared, then took Lil's hand and slowly guided her out of the pyramid, not a soul daring to stop them. Outside, Raviel and Lil quickened their return to the speeder. Lil was silent until they arrived. Raviel went to sit in the driver's seat, and Lil didn't object. They quickly strapped into the cockpit and secured the canopy. Lil looked over at Raviel.

"No one has ever dared confront the Prime Sanctums...you are indeed the Navi."

Raviel looked over at Lil, still trying to process what she was feeling without memory to help her.

"Maybe you don't have a past," Lil offered soberly. "Maybe you were created as you are, for this very time in history, for the good people of Rayl."

Raviel considered Lil's words. They were lonely purposeful words, but perhaps true words. Raviel tapped the controls. The speeder lifted up and away from this place of blasphemy. *Are these people even worth saving?* Raviel asked herself. She glanced toward Lil who had not yet taken her eyes from off of Raviel. Some were.

CHAPTER

4

The Zeal of Ell Yon

"Your enemies will remain among you to test your hearts, to discover if you will follow the ways of Ell Yon." ~Navi of the Haynian Occupation

When Raviel and Lil arrived at her home, it was evening, and the rush of their encounter had diminished. Raviel was still fighting to find her identity, if she had one. The fury of her reaction to the Raylean people that had dedicated their lives to Deitum Prime absorption surprised her. Why? She wondered. The whispers of Ell Yon had guided her, but the passion came from deep within her without effort, and yet she found herself becoming extremely frustrated as she pondered the absence of a past. Did Lil's speculation about her existence have any merit? The more she thought about who she might be, the more it frightened her. Was she a good person? Was she a criminal escaping a punishment? A mother...a wife...a daughter? Her thoughts turned back to the encounter at the Prime Pyramid. A combatant! Her subconscious mind and muscle memory knew exactly how to take out multiple threats at once.

Definitely a combatant of some sort, she concluded.

Raviel stepped out of the speeder, but Lil had already bolted up to the entrance of their home. The property was positioned on the outskirts of the city with a bit of land to sustain a garden and a few animals. As a chieftain, Lil's father would have surely been afforded more luxuries than what was evident here. Raviel took note and assumed there would be a measure of humility in the man. She walked slowly up to the open door, not sure if she should enter. She lingered then heard the commotion and voices of multiple people within. A moment later, Lil appeared with a stout man behind her, quickly followed by Lil's mother, and four younger siblings. Raviel attempted a smile, but she didn't feel much like pretending. Lil went to Raviel's side and put her arm through Raviel's arm.

"This is the woman I told you about," she said with reserved enthusiasm. Lil's father scrutinized Raviel with narrow eyes. After a few seconds, he held out his arm.

"I am Panodin, and this is my wife, Shatril. Please, miss, come in and have a meal with us."

Shortly after the awkward greeting was over, Raviel was seated at a large table with Lil's family of seven. The aroma and sight of the delicious food before her was overwhelming as she realized that she was still famished from whatever ordeal she had experienced. Perhaps her stomach had never had food in it before. Once Panodin finished offering thanks to Ell Yon for their provisions, the meal began. Raviel was grateful that they allowed her some time to finish most of the meal before the questions came.

"What is your name and where do you hail from?" Panodin asked.

With clearly much anticipation, the rest of Lil's family became still, waiting for her answer. Raviel wiped her lips with her napkin, setting it beside her clean plate. She looked at Shatril.

"Thank you for the delicious meal. I was famished." She offered a subtle smile then looked toward Panodin.

"I'm afraid I don't know the answer to either of those questions. It seems the beginning of my memories start when Lil found me lying on the floor."

"Floor?" one of Lil's brothers asked.

"At the Navi Hall of Meditation," Lil piped in. "In the very center as is foretold by the oracles." Lil's eyes lifted. "She's the Navi, Father!"

Panodin held up his hand. "Lil...let's not jump to such extreme conclus—"

"But she wears the Protector, and I saw —"

"Lil!" Panodin scolded.

Lil frowned just short of scowling, then calmed herself. Panodin turned his gaze to Raviel's arm.

"Where did you get that?" he asked, nodding toward Raviel's arm. A sliver of silver hinted at something priceless beneath the fabric of her sleeve. Raviel pulled back the sleeve revealing the glimmering glory of the Protector which incited a sense of awe and wonder by the entire family, including Panodin.

Raviel lifted her arm up, turning her hand back and forth as if to inspect its intricate design. She slowly shook her head.

"I don't know," she said pursing her lips.

"May I see it?" Panodin asked, holding out his hand.

Raviel pulled back her arm, cradling the vambrace next to her stomach. The Protector was her only anchor. The thought of existing without it even for a moment was unbearable. Her eyes darkened.

"No."

Panodin's left eyebrow lifted. He slowly withdrew his hand.

"The people of Rayl have only one Protector," he said, further scrutinizing the one she was wearing. "And although there are legends of a second, it's difficult to believe that it would appear on the arm of a woman with no name and no past. I hope you can appreciate that as the Keeper of the Protector, I must be cautious."

"Who wears the Protector you keep?" Raviel asked.

Panodin's gaze lowered. He seemed to struggle with an answer.

"No one," Lil offered.

Raviel's heart stirred once more. At the city courtyard it was anger, here it was disappointment. Her brow furrowed. "Why?"

"No one dares lest they be found unworthy," Panodin said quietly. "As Lil has told you, it's why our people are in such despair with our enemies gathering against us. We have no leader to speak the voice of Ell Yon."

Raviel stared at the man. Silence hung in the air as the sober reality of Panodin's truthful words lingered.

"We went to one of the Prime Sanctums," Lil declared, breaking the silence.

"What?" Panodin and Shatril exclaimed simultaneously. Lil's siblings gawked at her with mouths open. Lil swallowed hard, garnering the strength for a full confession.

"We were attacked, but the Navi defeated them with the Protector. No one dared to touch us, and she rebuked them openly." Lil's gaze turned to Raviel, her eyes full of admiration. She then looked back at her parents. "She *is* the Navi Rayl has been waiting for, Father. I've seen it with my own eyes."

The entire family seemed stunned by Lil's testimony.

"If what Lil says is true, you must take her to see the Council," Shatril said quietly.

It was difficult to read Panodin's expression. The absence of words of retribution or opinion was evidently something new for his family as they all stared at him...waiting. His eyes darted from Shatril to Lil to Raviel until he stood and exited the room without saying a word. The awkward silence that followed was finally broken by Shatril with an attempt at alternative polite conversation.

With nowhere for Raviel to go, Shatril arranged a place for her to stay with them. Raviel spent the remainder of the evening watching the family and pondering her own fate.

The next day, after the morning meal, Panodin asked Raviel to join him outside on the terrace. The view in one direction was filled with lush vegetation, open plains, and a distant forest. To their left was the city of Jalem just a few miles away.

Panodin hesitated as he looked toward Jalem.

"It's our custom to offer kindness to travelers that are themselves honorable."

He paused, and Raviel waited.

"But I find it difficult to believe that you don't remember anything about who you are or where you've come from." He turned and glared at Raviel. "Lil is an idealistic dreamy girl, willing to believe any fanciful story with a hint of truth in it, but I am a realist. Enough of the charade. Who are you?"

Raviel turned and squared off with Panodin. "Sir, I wish I could remember, but I don't. All I can tell you is that something deep inside me is telling me I'm supposed to be here, and that Ell Yon is with me."

Panodin frowned, shaking his head. "That's not good enough. You put my daughter in harm's way yesterday, and that's something I can't overlook. Based on that, I think you're a threat to my family and you must leave."

Raviel turned and leaned against the rail of the terrace...thinking...listening.

You are here for such a time as this. Ell Yon's voice was unmistakable. Although she didn't know what the situation was with her people, the whispers of Ell Yon were always true.

"As you wish," Raviel said, then she turned her head toward him. "But you had better understand this...there's a much greater threat than I coming to this place and to your family. I see cowardice in the eyes of Rayl and disbelief in their hearts. Ell Yon is angry and unless our people turn to him, they will all be enslaved within the next thirty days."

Raviel straightened and looked Panodin in the eye, then turned to leave. At the threshold of the door, Panodin called out.

"Please stop!"

Raviel turned about, her eyes lit with the flame of Ell Yon. Panodin took a couple of steps toward her, his eyes filled with a new kind of fear.

"If you're willing, I'll take you to the Council of Chieftains."

Raviel cocked her head to one side, confused by his sudden change of heart. "What changed your mind?" she asked.

Panodin pointed to her arm. Raviel slowly lifted her right arm up. The Protector was aglow with blue flames angrily dancing across its surface.

"I've never seen the Protector react so." Panodin shook his head. "None dare wear it for fear of its power. For you to be able to wear it and bear such power with ease is evidence enough for me that you're telling the truth and that you've been sent by him." Panodin's gaze fell to the floor. "Everything you've said about our people is true. The Kaynians have already conquered six of our clans. Even as we speak, they are amassing forces across the river. Other chieftains are negotiating their surrender so as to minimize loss of life."

Raviel could feel her anger rising, an autonomic response at hearing such words of defeat. She returned to Panodin.

"Who sits on the council and what is the condition of our people?" she asked.

Over the course of the next three hours, Panodin briefed Raviel on the political and military status of the planet from both a historical and present-day perspective. Raviel learned that there were three major continents occupied by seven different nations. The Rayleans had conquered and occupied the largest continent, thereby renaming the planet Rayl. Many cities were built, and the population of the Raylean people was nearing fifty million, but as they had grown, they had walked away from the ways of Ell Yon.

On the eastern shores of the Raylean continent, an isthmus spanned a 75-mile stretch of land that connected to the next largest continent which was occupied by the original inhabitants of the planet, the

Kaynians. Viewing the Rayleans as off-world invaders, there was continual conflict between these two nations. The five other nations that occupied Rayl were the Domians, the Moians, the Midians, the Amians, and the Fillians. Though these people were each diverse in many ways, they all had one bond that united them...they all hated the Rayleans. Decades ago, the Kaynians had risen to power by allying themselves with other off-world powers which gave them access to technology and military might not afforded to the other nations on Rayl. For the past twenty years the Kaynians had advanced across the isthmus into Raylean territory, conquering and subduing six of the twelve Raylean clans and over half of the continent. They had increased their military might to that of a full invasion force with the intention of eradicating the planet of all Rayleans. The Shikon River was all that separated the Kaynians from the remaining free lands of the Rayleans. Panodin's portrayal of their situation was dismal. At one point he looked apologetically at Raviel.

"The prefect of Kayn is a man by the name of Binja and his commanding general is a ruthless man named Sisero. They have amassed over 900 assault craft and 120,000 soldiers. He's threatening total decimation of the Raylean people unless we unconditionally surrender and give him all of our possessions and our lands." Panodin wrung his hands. "If you're here by accident, then I'm afraid you're doomed with us. If you're here by Ell Yon's hand then we're going to need Immortal intervention just to survive."

"What is the status of our tech orders?"

"Paltry," Panodin returned. "Any buildup of our forcetech and aerotech orders was met with threats from the other nations and besides this, our twelve clans are not unified. We've never been able to establish a central cohesive leadership or government. There's simply too much division within the clans."

Raviel shook her head. "Division and Deitum Prime. It's a wonder we still exist at all."

Panodin wore lines of worry across his brow. Raviel reached across the table putting a hand on his arm.

"Take heart, Panodin. Ell Yon has not abandoned his people. He will give us victory over the Kaynians."

Panodin looked as if he was waiting for the punch line to a bad joke. Hope was still far from his heart.

"I wish I could be as sanguine as you," he replied, his eyes becoming distant with despair. Raviel stood up. She needed time to process all she'd heard.

"When does the Council of Chieftains meet next?" Raviel asked.

"Tomorrow. Each Chieftain is allowed an accompanying executive assistant. I'll take you as mine."

"Very well," she agreed. "Tomorrow."

5

The Acumen
of a Navi

"In the days of sorrow, a Navi shall suddenly appear
and lead them, and the boot of their oppressor shall
be lifted." -Darnullay, Oracle of Ell Yon

As Panodin and Raviel entered Jalem, the glittering towers shifted to gray once more as the spewing columns of misted Deitum Prime saturated the city with its dark influence. Raviel's heart began to beat hard within her chest, not for fear but for judgment.

Panodin set his craft down on the western edge of the city's inner court. They walked toward the tallest building, but Raviel couldn't dislodge her gaze from the four Prime Pyramids 100 yards to her left. She felt the Protector surging with fierce power.

Once inside the building, they mounted an anti-grav platform that lifted them up through a wide and open concourse reaching 112 stories high. With just a thin rail between the rising platform and the open concourse, it made Raviel's stomach churn the higher they rose. As the anti-grav platform slowed and came to a stop, a walkway extended outward toward them. They exited across the walkway and entered a large conference room surrounded by glass walls that offered a truly majestic view, but the glamour of it all was overshadowed by desperate times.

Twelve curved tables were positioned like the numbers on a clock around the center of the room, with space between each table to allow access to the inner section.

Panodin walked to his seat at the table with a placard labeled "Leevok" and sat down. Six of the tables, those identified as Simak, Galloway, Revitar, Joshe, Azuran, and Isak were present but had no chieftain sitting at them. Each sitting chieftain had an executive assistant standing behind and to the right of him or her. Raviel took a similar position behind Panodin once he was seated. The other chieftains scrutinized her.

"What is she doing here?" Luas, the chieftain of the Zealon clan demanded. He was young, not much older than Raviel, but he was often the most outspoken of the chieftains. "The Council of Chieftains is exclusive, Panodin, you know this! She is not an authorized executive assistant."

"As chieftain of the Leevok Clan and Keeper of the Protector, it is my duty to inform all other chieftains of any unusual circumstances regarding the Immortal device," Panodin proclaimed, attempting to rally himself to stand against the forceful personalities of Luas, Korban, and Tialla.

The other five chieftains glanced from one to another.

Korban leaned forward. "What unusual circumstances? No one has dared attempt to fasten themselves to it since Navi Yar over 120 years ago."

"Or is it that you've lost it?" Tialla chided. This brought chuckles from two of the other chieftains.

Panodin lifted the case he was carrying and set it on the table. He pressed a sequence of buttons, and the top of the case slid open from its center point in all directions revealing the priceless treasure of the Rayleans. Sight of the Immortal tech instantly evoked a silent awe from all in the room. Raviel glanced from chieftain to chieftain, stunned by their reactions.

"What good does it do if no one wears it?" Raviel blurted out. "How can you possibly know the voice of Ell Yon without it?"

Luas stood, fury on his face. "Silence!" he shouted, pointing his finger at her. "Irrelevants do not speak here nor should they be in our presence!" he continued, flashing a glare toward Panodin.

Luas, Korban, and Tialla looked indignant, but the other chieftains appeared stunned and influenced by her bold words.

"She's right, Chieftain Luas. Ell Yon has abandoned us," Chieftain Vansan from the Jahrim clan said quietly.

"True," added another. "Even now the Kaynians are gathering their forces on the eastern shores of the Shikon River to retake the remaining land we stole from them."

"We're doomed," continued Vansan. "The Kaynians outnumber us two-to-one and they have a fleet of attack craft against which we have virtually no defenses. Where is Ell Yon now? Where is the leader who dares don the Protector and hear his voice?"

Raviel's heart began to seethe with disgust as the impuissant ranting of the chieftains continued. Although her past was void of any concise memory, the essence of who she was and what she was called to was vibrantly evident in her beating heart.

Raviel stepped forward beside Panodin which made him extremely anxious. She glared about the room letting the fury of her countenance rest on the faces of each of the chieftains.

"Your brothers and sisters are under the tyrannical rule of Binja and Sisero and you do nothing! They're coming for you...all of you!" she exclaimed, sweeping an accusing finger across them all. "You are conquered because you've turned away from Sovereign Ell Yon and have filled your bellies with Deitum Prime. It's shameful!" Raviel stepped into the center of the room, unable to stop the chastisement flowing from the Protector and through her lips. "What is wrong with all of you? This is not your destiny...this is not your future!" her voice continued to rise in volume. "Have you all become spineless doubters of Sovereign Ell Yon so quickly?"

At that, Luas walked briskly toward her, fury filling his countenance. "Silence, Irrelevant!" he said grabbing her left arm. "Guards! Take her—"

Luas's words were cut short as Raviel opened the palm of her right hand and the Protector burst to life. One short brilliant pulse of energy slammed into his chest which sent him flying over his table, across the room, and up against the wall. He crumbled to a heap on the floor. Two council guards aimed their plasma rifles at her, and she turned to face them. Before they could fire, a broad burst from the Protector slammed them up against the wall, momentarily suspended until Raviel closed her hand, releasing them. They too fell unconscious to the floor. With the fire of Ell Yon in her eyes, Raviel turned to face the remaining five chieftains and their assistants, all now cowering behind their tables.

"She wears the...a Protector!" Vansan whispered.

"A Navi?" Tialla asked sheepishly of the two chieftains next to her.

Raviel glared at the chieftains, the Protector pulsing waves of anger across the jeweled ribbons and throughout her synaptic connection.

"Wake him and bring him to the table," she ordered, pointing to the crumpled form of Luas.

Three chieftains quickly obeyed, splashing water on Luas's face. He was slow to recover but when he did, fear and astonishment filled his eyes as he looked toward Raviel.

"Your lack of faith in Ell Yon is repulsive," Raviel berated. She walked about the inner circle of tables, gazing deep into the eyes of each attending chieftain. They all cowered, their gaze ever on the gleaming angry Protector she held out before them. When she reached Panodin's table she lifted the other Protector out of its case, holding it before them.

"Is there no one among you who can wear the Protector?" she asked. "Is there no one worthy?" She frowned. "Or is it that the Protector rejects you because you are all guilty of immersing yourselves in the pleasures of Deitum Prime?"

All of the chieftains lowered their eyes in shame.

"You wonder where Ell Yon is in your time of desperation, and yet you live as hypocrites. This is why Ell Yon has not given you the entire planet of Rayl. This is why the Kaynians are threatening your existence. Ell Yon has allowed it because of your foolish hearts and fickle faith in him. I know not where I come from, but I do know this...I am here to tell you that Sovereign Ell Yon has not abandoned you nor is his power so limited, as many of you have come to believe, that he cannot deliver you from this evil army!"

Raviel rotated to see if there was even one chieftain that had the smallest measure of courage.

"Why did you meet as a Council of Chieftains today? Was it to agree to terms of surrender? Perhaps to make plans to flee the planet?"

Silence was her response. She turned and looked into the eyes of Panodin.

"This must be a council of war, and you must lead our people now!"

"But how, Navi?" Panodin asked. "We're not prepared, and it's you who wears the Protector." Panodin glanced quickly toward the other chieftains. "You must lead us."

"Yes," exclaimed another. "We've waited for a Navi for over a century. You must lead us!"

Raviel shook her head, disappointment spilling from her heart. She waited for the whisper of Ell Yon and it came.

"I will lead you, but know this...history will reveal the cowardice of the chieftains to all future generations of Rayl...that an obscure woman will have risen up to lead when there was no one else with a heart of courage."

She scanned the faces once more, looking for a rebuttal, but there was none.

"So let it be," Luas said.

"So let it be," followed the unified voices of the other chieftains.

"What do we do?" Panodin asked.

Raviel carefully placed the other Protector back in its case then turned to face the chieftains.

"We prepare for war, but first we turn our hearts back to Sovereign Ell Yon." Her brow furrowed. "If I lead you, there is no turning back, and you will support the directives of Ell Yon without question." She looked right at Luas. "Am I understood?"

All at once the Protector threatened to unleash its energy with vibrant powerful bursts of blue flames. Luas knelt to one knee and the others followed. Raviel knelt to one knee along with the chieftains and held the Protector high above her, an umbrella of fierce power filling the room.

"As you have said, so pledge we," Luas said.

The fame of the arrival of a Navi spread quickly. With fearless resolve, Raviel first destroyed the Prime Sanctums in every Raylean city and those that defended them. She struggled to hide her utter disdain for the fickle Rayleans that were so easily beset by the lures of Deitum Prime. Her bold actions to destroy the Sanctums triggered a national period of deep sorrow for having abandoned the ways of Ell Yon for so long, but they also brought fierce threats from many not willing to abandon their pernicious ways. Much to Raviel's disdain, the chieftains insisted on protecting her with an entourage of security every hour of every day. Ironically, Chieftain Luas became her most ardent defender and supporter. Though time was short, and their enemies were gathering, Raviel knew that their only path forward was a nationwide return to their Sovereign. When their time of sorrow was complete, Raviel stepped forward to lead her people to victory.

There were moments during the first few weeks when Raviel's passion for her people and for Sovereign Ell Yon surprised even her. It felt strange to be so deeply motivated and to carry such intense convictions without some basis for which they existed. At times this was maddening for her, but slowly she simply allowed her passions to exist and to guide her as she received counsel from the Protector. One thing was certain...she was fully aligned with the Protector which diminished the need to justify her emotions and actions. She knew that eventually, her current experiences might very well be the whole of her memories and the essence of what defined her. In the throes of preparation for war, there was peace within for this pursuit. It was only in the still of the night that she occasionally found that peace elusive as she contemplated her final role in this saga of Rayl.

On the twenty-fifth day of her arrival, Raviel called for a council of the six remaining chieftains and their forcetech, aerotech, and scitech commanders. In short order, Raviel discovered that there was absolutely no military strategy that would win the day with the Kaynians. Chieftains Luas of the Zealon clan and Tialla of the Nasher clan were the only two that had any semblance of military assets. The other four clans were sheep to the slaughter.

"How can we possibly defend ourselves against the Kaynians with such a paltry force?" Luas asked cautiously. "They are amassing their forces along the Shikon River, and I fear will attack any day. They aren't even asking to negotiate. I suspect they intend on total decimation."

Raviel was at a loss as to how to respond. There indeed seemed no possible defense against such a massive force.

I will deliver them into your hand, the whisper came.

Raviel stepped into the inner ring of the council tables. She turned to capture the gaze of all eighteen leaders in the room. Fear and apprehension laced the countenance of them all, but also deep respect for the one who had brought them back to Ell Yon.

"We aren't going to defend ourselves from the Kaynians," Raviel proclaimed. None dared respond, having learned the fierceness of rebuke for a show of timidity. "We're going to attack, for Ell Yon has promised victory."

The chieftains and tech commanders glanced from one to another in astonishment, but Raviel wasn't finished.

"We will crush the Kaynians and retake our land and our people from their hand!"

"Forgive me, Navi," Tialla dared interrupt. "How and with what forces? You've just heard the condition of our aerotech and forcetech orders."

Raviel glared back at Tialla who winced.

"This is not a battle to win a plot of ground. This is a battle for our survival. Tomorrow at dawn, I want every able-bodied Raylean that has ever fired a plasma rifle and every craft that can fly to assemble on the western banks of the Shikon River. The Kaynians have an army of 120,000 soldiers. We will assemble an army of 500,000."

Raviel let her words settle in the hearts of her commanders.

"They'll see us coming," one forcetech commander said.

"Yes...let them see us coming," Raviel returned. She turned to the scitech masters. "I'm assuming you can tap into the Kaynians communications network?"

"Yes, we already have," replied Luas's scitech master. "They're not even trying to hide their intentions."

"Good, and neither will we. Let them hear of our call for 500,000 soldiers and let them clearly hear that the Immortal Ell Yon is with us and has already declared our victory."

The scitechs smiled. "We will begin immediately."

"Navi." Chieftain Korban stood and bowed. "The Kaynians have many weapon systems, but our intelligence sources claim that one weapon they have acquired off world is most concerning...laser-guided high energy delta missiles."

"Continue," Raviel replied.

Chieftain Korban turned to his forcetech commander and nodded. The commander stood and cleared his throat.

"The intent of the missile is ghastly...to destroy only macro animal biology while leaving the plant-based ecosystem and infrastructure unharmed. It does so by detonating just above the surface emitting high intensity delta particles out to a radius of 2,000 feet. As you know, although delta particles only exist for a few seconds, they annihilate living tissue in microseconds. Any person within the blast radius will be dissolved in an instant."

"By our estimates," Chieftain Korban continued, "they have over 1,200 delta missiles at their disposal, and they intend to use them. We could lose 100,000 lives in the first few minutes of the battle."

The council chamber became soberly silent. Raviel bowed her head, listening, but the Protector was silent. Slowly she lifted her eyes to Chieftain Korban. He swallowed hard, waiting for her response. She turned to Chieftain Luas.

"Assemble our army."

"As you wish, Navi."

5

Not Alone

O rders to mobilize the masses went forth, and the people responded with great enthusiasm, for the presence of a Navi gave them courage. Luas, Korban, and Tialla established a tactical headquarters in a town 8 miles from the Shikon River to coordinate the arriving forces. Within HQ there was a bustle of constant activity as Raviel received situation reports from the aerotech, forcetech, and scitech leaders.

"Chieftain Luas, you will lead the attack tomorrow," Raviel declared.

"If you'll be with me, I'll do as you request," Luas replied.

Raviel offered a crooked smile. "Don't worry...I'll be there."

Luas nodded, then tilted his head. "Please excuse me, Navi, I need to attend to a matter." He exited the command center then returned a few minutes later. He looked concerned.

"What is it?" Raviel asked.

"Two unidentified off-world craft have landed near the city of Jalem."

"Detain them until this is over. We don't have time to deal with this now," Raviel said hastily, returning to a new set of reports she'd just been handed on a glass tablet.

Luas hesitated. "They claim to be Rayleans and are offering to help fight the battle tomorrow."

At that Raviel paused, then shook her head. "It could be a trick. The timing is too convenient."

"I agree, Navi," Luas returned, "but if they're telling the truth we could use all of the air support we can get, and their craft look very capable." Luas flicked an image from his glass to the 3D table which displayed the craft in detail. Raviel huffed then nodded.

"They're requesting an audience with you," Luas added.

"Very well. Bring them."

"As you wish, Navi. I'll verify genetic scans first and post extra security."

Raviel smirked as she glanced toward the four soldiers already standing nearby. "Is that really necessary?"

Luas pretended not to hear her as he exited HQ once more. Thirty minutes later, he returned with six more security guards escorting two men, a woman and an android.

To say that Daeson was concerned for Raviel was a gross understatement. His spacetime wrist band indicated that they had overshot Raviel's arrival here by almost a month. The missing clothes and Talon certainly indicated that she had arrived, but he hadn't been able to discover her whereabouts or her medical condition. The four of them had travelled over 400 years into the future to find her. It was a number that frightened him. What would such a spacetime anomaly do to her already fragile biological condition? And besides the apprehension of not knowing the condition of his bonded soulmate, they had arrived just in time to witness what appeared to be the impending decimation of the entire Raylean population. Word that a powerful Navi was leading them offered hope, but Daeson's memory of Admiral Bostra as a former leader of the people gave him pause. Bostra had worn the Protector too, but it did little to keep them from near eradication. After too much delay, they had finally been granted an audience.

Daeson, Tig, Kyrah, and Rivet had been given strict instructions on the proper manner in which to address the Navi which further concerned Daeson.

"Sounds like this Navi thinks too highly of himself," Daeson said quietly. "I can't imagine Sovereign Ell Yon allowing much of that."

Due to the urgency of the situation, the four of them were brought directly to the tactical headquarters. They entered to see a frenzy of activity, especially around the four center tables where 3D graphic displays were offering visuals on the gathering forces. They were halted just inside the large room, watching. Finally, they were brought within fifteen feet of one of the command tables where a group of men and women were gathered. The man escorting them turned to face Daeson.

"Wait here," he said sternly, scrutinizing them once more. "You'd better be true to your word. The Navi will know."

The man left and worked his way through the group of commanders in front of them. Daeson tried to see which man wore the Protector but couldn't make him out. The man bent over and whispered into the ear of a woman whose back was to them. She turned about, and Daeson's heart nearly stopped. Raviel fastened her eyes on him. He nearly called out, but something stayed his tongue. Perhaps it was the look in her eyes or the way in which she seemed to control her own emotions. Was this situation such that she dared not reveal her understanding of who they were? He wondered. Her eyes were completely devoid of recognition. Was this a ploy? His heart quickened as she slowly stepped toward them. Four guards stayed close by, ready to act at the slightest hint of threat to their Navi.

"Navi, these are the pilots I told you about earlier," the man who had escorted them said.

Tig and Kyrah looked to Daeson for some sign of how to react. He offered one slight shake of his head. Raviel stepped to within a few feet of them, carefully examining each one in turn. When she examined Rivet, she paused.

"You're unusual...not like the other bots here."

Rivet stayed silent and still. Raviel then turned to Daeson, Tig, and Kyrah, placing her hands on her hips. Daeson nearly smiled. He had seen that stance many times before. It was a posture of confident determination. He caught just a glimpse of the lower edge of the Protector on her right forearm and was instantly satisfied. He would play the part she needed him to play.

"Chieftain Luas tells me you have craft that will help us in this fight," Raviel said.

"That's correct," Daeson returned. "I understand your situation is rather desperate. We're loyal Rayleans and will do whatever we can to help."

Raviel's eyes narrowed. "Your craft are military. Where do you come from and why have you been off world?"

Daeson paused. She wasn't making this easy. He glanced at the man she called Luas.

"Some time ago, we were trained in the Jyptonian aerotech forces. Once we heard of the condition of our people, we were able to acquire a couple of older Starcrafts and make our way here. Our forcetech training will be a great asset to you."

Raviel looked skeptical. "Your scans identify you as Raylean. If you betray us, you will be executed," she stated coldly.

Daeson's eyes raised. This was a side of Raviel he'd never seen before. He was trying to adapt as quickly as possible. "You have our word. Our lives are in your hands."

Raviel began to turn away.

"Navi, you're not alone here. May I have a word with you in private?" Daeson asked.

Luas's countenance became fierce. "Absolutely not!"

Raviel turned back and held up her hand, which seemed to instantly tame the man. Her eyes narrowed once more.

"I don't think that's necessary. I have my questions answered, and you can have yours answered in the aerotech briefings which will begin in thirty minutes." Raviel turned her back on them, and the guards stepped between her and Daeson just as a young woman entered the room and came to Raviel. Daeson saw Raviel put an arm around the lass and walk away from the rest of the commanders to allow a confidential discussion.

Daeson turned to look at Tig and Kyrah. They looked as stunned as he felt. There was a sinking feeling in the pit of his stomach that something was horribly wrong.

After the three pilots and the android departed, Raviel turned to Luas. "There's something peculiar about them...keep your eye on them."

Luas nodded. "Agreed."

Outside HQ, Daeson, Tig, Kyrah, and Rivet found a secluded place to talk.

"That was strange," Tig said.

Daeson nodded. "There must be a reason she needed us to appear disconnected from her. A lot must have happened in the three weeks she's been here."

"I'll say," Kyrah added. "The regard those commanders have for her is a level of respect I've never seen before. She did something to earn such devotion so quickly."

Daeson was lost in thought, trying hard to understand what was happening. Her training as a Nexus spy back on Jypton was serving her well. There wasn't even a fraction of a moment that she dropped out of character.

"We need more information," Daeson declared.

"I don't think anyone close to her is going to talk to us right now," Tig said. "And she made it clear that she isn't going to give anything."

"Perhaps we should ask her," Rivet interrupted, turning his head toward the doors of the headquarters building. A young woman had just exited, and she was none too happy. She huffed, crossed her arms, and began pacing, muttering something to herself.

"Why her?" Kyrah asked.

"Raviel's actions toward the girl indicated a protective affection," Rivet replied. "And her words indicated the same. I believe the girl has been with Raviel from the beginning."

Daeson looked at Rivet. "And how do you know that? We weren't close enough to hear anything."

Rivet tilted his head in his usual way. "You weren't, my liege, but I was. My audio telescopic listening sensors were able to isolate and capture forty-three seconds of their conversation. The girl's name is Lil, and she wants to join the battle, but Raviel won't allow it."

"Rivet, once again you continue to amaze," Daeson said with a smile. "Kyrah, you approach first."

"Got it." Kyrah made her way toward the door as if on an errand, then pretended to notice Lil off to the side.

"You okay?" she asked.

The girl startled, clearly absorbed in her episode of frustration.

"What? Oh...yeah...I'm fine," Lil replied.

"Hey," Kyrah exclaimed with a smile as she walked toward Lil, "aren't you the one who knows the Navi so well?"

Lil flashed a quick smile then smirked.

"A lot of good that does me. Looks like I'm going to miss the greatest battle of the ages."

Kyrah warmed up to Lil. "How so?"

Lil seemed encouraged by having a listener for her woes. "My father has forbidden me to join with the entire Raylean population to fight against the Kaynians, and the Navi is siding with him."

"I'm sorry," Kyrah sympathized. "If you don't mind me asking, how do you know the Navi so well?"

By now Daeson, Tig and Rivet had stepped up beside Kyrah. Lil eyed them.

"It's okay," Kyrah assured her, "they're with me. We're pilots that are going to fight in the battle tomorrow."

Lil's eyes opened wide. "You're the off-world pilots that came to help! I've heard about you."

"That's us," Daeson said offering his hand. "This is Kyrah, Tig, and our bot Rivet."

"I'm Lil. You're for real, aren't you?" she asked. "There are lots of rumors going around about you."

"We're for real," Daeson replied. "Sovereign Ell Yon led us here, and we'll give everything to the fight to save his people."

Lil seemed mesmerized by Daeson's warm gaze. "You have the same fire in your eyes as the Navi."

"How do you know her?" he asked.

"Know her...I found her," Lil offered.

"Incredible! Where did she come from?"

Lil took a deep breath. "I often go the Navi Hall of Meditation to think. It's abandoned now since most everyone had given up on the hope of the legend of a Navi appearing there. One afternoon I went there, and she was just lying in the middle of the hall, like she had appeared out of nowhere."

Daeson feigned surprise as he listened to Lil's rendition of the events of Raviel's arrival. "So where *did* she come from?" he pressed.

"She says she can't remember, and no one here has ever seen her before so it is possible. Perhaps Ell Yon brought her from the Ruah. She has no name, no home, no past. She's here to save us from the Kaynians, that's all I know."

Daeson's spirit began to falter. He looked at Tig and Kyrah, seeing the same concern on their faces.

"No past?" Daeson asked. "You mean she doesn't remember anything? She has no memory at all?"

Lil nodded. "I don't think she ever *had* a memory. Like I said, maybe she's Ell Yon's creation just to save our nation from this evil army of Sisero."

Daeson's chest began to hurt. If what Lil said was true, it was possible that the spacetime anomaly had wiped her memory clean. He clung to the hope that her memory loss was temporary.

"Does she hear Ell Yon's whispers through the Protector?" Tig asked.

Lil's eyes lifted. "Oh yes! I watched her use the Protector to blast a man clear across the room...in one of the Prime Sanctums. Father said she did the same thing to one of the chieftains and two guards at the Council of Chieftains gathering. Every living Raylean adores her...well...the ones that follow Ell Yon at least." Lil hesitated. "I don't suppose you would be willing to speak to my father...you know...to convince him to let me fight tomorrow?"

Kyrah reached out and put a gentle hand on her shoulder. "If you're willing to trust the Navi with the fate of the Rayl, perhaps you should trust her in this regard too."

Lil's shoulders dropped.

"Don't worry, Lil," Kyrah said. "I'm sure there will be many great challenges for you to conquer soon."

Daeson immediately began searching for a way to help Raviel, even if she didn't think she needed it.

"Lil, where did the Navi get the Protector?" he asked.

"She was wearing it when I found her." Lil answered. "Which is why I immediately knew she was the Navi we've been waiting for. No one has worn our Protector for many decades."

"What do you mean, 'our Protector'?" Daeson probed.

"My father is the chieftain of the Leevok Clan and the Keeper of the Protector. When the Navi appeared with a second Protector—"

All of a sudden, Lil's eyes opened wide, and she took a step back.

"What's wrong, Lil?" Kyrah asked, trying to warm back up to the girl.

"I think I've said too much already. I'm not so sure my father would want me to be talking to you about this."

"It's okay," Daeson said. "You don't need to say anything more. We understand how important it is to keep the Protector secure."

Lil seemed to relax a bit after hearing that. Tig pulled Daeson away from Kyrah and the girl.

"You need to be wearing that Protector during the battle tomorrow," he whispered.

"Perhaps, but we run the risk of appearing malevolent and jeopardizing our involvement in the battle," Daeson returned.

"Tig is correct," Rivet added, stepping beside them. "I believe the young woman can be trusted."

"What do you mean, 'I can be trusted'?" Lil raised her voice, looking over Kyrah's shoulder.

"Can I ask you one more question?" Daeson asked returning to Lil. "And it has nothing to do with the Protector."

"I guess," Lil said rubbing her arm.

Daeson lowered his head slightly, gazing deeply into Lil's eyes. "Why were you really at the Hall of Mediation the day you found the Navi?"

Lil seemed captured by Daeson's gaze. She hesitated, seeming to choose her words carefully. "My father says I'm a dreamer, taken to believe in fanciful tales." Lil looked away toward the Shikon River where tomorrow's battle would take place. "Perhaps I *am* just that, because I dream of a better life for my people than what they're living." She looked back at Daeson. "I was at the hall because it's where I feel the closest to Sovereign Ell Yon, and I believe him when he promises to deliver us from our enemies. For me, that's more than a dream. That's why I want to fight with my people tomorrow."

Daeson smiled. "The eyes of Ell Yon search throughout the whole galaxy for hearts such as yours."

Lil gave Daeson a scrutinizing look. "I heard him whisper something about the Protector," Lil said glancing Tig's way. "What do you want with it?"

Daeson, Tig, and Kyrah all exchanged glances.

"Lil," Kyrah began. "Very few people would believe us if we told them who we really are, and besides this, we don't have time." Kyrah put a gentle hand on Lil's elbow. "As the Navi is, this man once was. He wore the Protector that your Navi is now wearing."

Lil looked at Daeson out of the corner of her eye.

"If he were to wear the Protector your father keeps tomorrow, imagine what that might mean for our people," Kyrah continued.

Lil seemed lost in thought as she considered Kyrah's words.

"The Navi that you admire and love," Daeson added, "we do too. She's one of us, but she doesn't remember because of the tragedy that brought her here."

She turned to face Daeson straight on, looking deeply into his eyes.

"I see it," she said quietly. "But there's no way that my father or any of the other chieftains would allow it without a full vetting of who you are."

"I know," Daeson said. "With or without the Protector, we're going to fight in that battle for our people. If there is anything you can do to help us..." Daeson hesitated.

Lil stiffened. "I think I can help."

Daeson nodded. "You are part of the remnant that never turned away from your faith in the Sovereign. You and those like you are why Ell Yon has not abandoned us."

Lil smiled. "I'll meet you after the briefings," she said then turned and disappeared into the night.

The three of them looked on after her.

"Do think she really believes us?" Tig asked. "What if she doesn't and takes her concerns to the chieftains?"

"Her biological scans did indicate elevated heart rate and blood pressure," Rivet said.

"I trust her," Kyrah countered.

"I do too," Daeson added. "Our briefing starts in five minutes. Let's see what we're in for."

CHAPTER

7

The Battle for Rayl

Daeson, Tig, Kyrah, and Rivet found inconspicuous seats near the back of a small auditorium that was used as the briefing room. This briefing was for all of the aerotech pilots, but it would also be broadcast securely to as many civil craft as was possible. The rest of the pilots of the civil force would have to get their assignments later. There were over 500 men and women in the auditorium.

Chieftain Luas and his aerotech commander along with the commander from the Nasher Clan stood at the front of the assembly and began to brief their plan. Raviel was sitting to the side along with the other five chieftains.

"From our analysis of the Kaynian aero forces, the center of the conflict will be here. The Navi is planning to lead our forcetech troops on the ground, so I want a tactical formation of our ten frigates and six destroyers along this line to provide cover," Luas explained as a

3D graphic display came to life describing his strategy. Daeson noticed that Raviel looked frustrated.

"The purpose of your forces, Chieftain Luas, are not to protect me but to win the day," Raviel exclaimed.

"But, Navi, you must be protected. Your leadership is everything to our people in this time of trial."

"No!" Daeson shouted from the back of the room. "The Navi is right." Daeson stood and all eyes turned to him. "The perception of strength is a key part of the success of the Navi's plan."

"Silence!" Luas shouted. "Our aerotech strategists have carefully laid out a plan that we will follow," the chieftain rebuked. Other commanders voiced their affirmation.

"It's a bad plan!" Daeson shouted back.

"You're an off-worlder. What do you know?" shouted one of the commanders as the room erupted. Guards began moving toward Daeson, Tig, Kyrah, and Rivet. Raviel stood and locked her eyes on Daeson. She raised her hand and the room fell silent...still.

"Let him speak."

Daeson stepped out from his place and walked down the center aisle to the front of the auditorium, his eyes ever searching Raviel's for some hint of recognition, but all he saw was curiosity.

"Navi, you called hundreds of thousands of Raylean citizens to battle, many who have never seen combat. You called thousands of craft to the skies, both aerotech and civilian. We must present a perception of military might across our entire frontline. Concentrating our forcetech and aerotech forces in the center over you won't do that. Chieftain Luas, you must spread your fleet along with the forcetech craft from the Nasher Clan across the entire 150-mile frontline. And we need our scitechs to spoof their Kaynian radar systems by having as many civilian craft as possible squawking a military aerotech signature." Daeson looked at the commanders. "We need to quit thinking this is about surviving the day. It's about—"

"Victory and recovering our lands," Raviel interrupted. She walked toward Daeson, eyes narrow...questioning.

"But Navi," Luas began to protest.

Raviel broke her gaze from Daeson, turning to address the rest of the pilots and commanders.

"On this day and on every day following, there will no longer be Raylean citizens. Every man, woman, and child will put on the mindset of a warrior, for our enemies are all around us. Our forcetech people and assets will not be called to battle...our nation will be called to battle." She looked at Luas. "This man is right. Make it so!"

Luas bowed his head. "As you wish, Navi."

Raviel turned back to face Daeson, a fierce look in her eyes. "Assist them in developing this strategy. They will hear you now." She then abruptly exited the room.

Raviel exited the briefing room. Once outside, her stiff composure collapsed the moment the door closed behind her. She leaned up against the wall, trying to sort out what had just happened. From nowhere, deep feelings threatened to undo her. The words of the off-world pilot had synchronized perfectly with the Protector, but it was more than even that. There was something personal happening, and she didn't like it. Was this man someone from her past? Whatever he was, she didn't like how weak these feelings made her. There was too much at stake no matter what was happening. She took a deep breath, straightened her shoulders and set out to meet with the commander of the ground forces.

"General Hart, what's our status?" she asked as she entered the briefing room. The room immediately snapped to attention. "At ease...report."

General Hart was an older man with a stern countenance whose eyes at times betrayed his fierce demeanor. He looked overwhelmed, running his hand through his white and gray hair.

"Navi, we're doing our best, but the sheer number of people coming to the battle is staggering. If you're looking for some specific strategy, I have nothing to offer."

Raviel glanced at the displays showing the Shikon River and the gathering forces. Hart was right—over 500,000 Rayleans had gathered, and even more were coming. Her heart fainted at the sight. What if the Kaynian's delta missiles couldn't be stopped? It would be a massacre their nation could not recover from. She was stunned by the thought of it.

"Navi?" Hart questioned.

Raviel broke from her concentration of the display.

"Where are the Kaynian forces strongest?" she asked.

"Both their air and ground forces seem to be concentrated here," Hart said, pointing to a broad inward curve along the Shikon River.

Raviel nodded. "That matches with Luas's briefing. Very well. You and I will be there...at the front."

"Are you certain, Navi?" Hart asked, his eyes softening.

Raviel smiled, putting a reassuring hand on his arm. "Absolutely!"

Hart's eyes manifested the deep admiration and respect in his heart for his courageous Navi.

"The ground assault destroyer will be ready at zero 4:30."

Raviel nodded and left. She needed time to listen to the Protector and to be with Ell Yon. There was still so much yet unrevealed. After two hours of petitioning and one short hour of rest, all she had was his promise. She steeled herself for the battle—his promise was all she needed.

Raviel tied her hair to a single braid and donned the combat uniform Luas had arranged for her. It was fashioned after the marines of his clan, the Zealon clan, but it fit well with protective body armor from her ankles to her neck. The right sleeve had been shortened to allow for the Protector to be conspicuous and accessible. She fastened her Talon about her waist, checked that the charge on her plasma rifle was full, then packed two more power modules for it in her ammo vest. She set the com link in her ear and donned the lightweight night vision glasses. She stood in front of the full-length mirror, checking to make sure she was fully equipped.

A combatant indeed, she thought. This felt so natural that she knew such gear had to have been part of her past.

She exited her quarters and out onto the HQ yard where she was greeted by thousands...all waiting for her. Large lights illumined the compound and those that were there.

"For Ell Yon...and the Navi!" They shouted in unison. Raviel was stunned at the sight and sound of such adoration. It was overwhelming and humbling. Pilots, commanders, chieftains, scitechs, forcetechs... all had come to rally for the battle that loomed. Five hundred thousand more looked on via the scitech's visual telemetry network. The shattered pride of Rayl was healing.

"For Ell Yon...and the Navi," the chant continued, rising in volume with one unified voice.

Raviel didn't know how to respond. She searched the faces of her commanders and chieftains looking for help, but they were fully taken in by the rallying cry for victory. She noticed the android first, then the three off-world pilots next to him. They were standing at the front of the crowd just off to her right. Their leader was looking at her the same way he had in the briefing, as if he knew a secret no one else knew...not even her. It jarred her at first, but then the warmth of his gaze comforted her in the strangest of ways. He tapped his right arm then pointed to a concrete abutment.

Of course, she thought. Raviel flung the plasma rifle over her shoulder, then jumped up onto the abutment. She held up her right arm, the glimmering Protector raised high for all to see. The cheers erupted to a heightened level then subsided as she opened her hand.

"Sovereign Ell Yon sent me to you at the edge of your destruction, oppressed by the evil ways of the Kaynians. I called you back to Ell Yon and you came. You humbled yourselves before the Immortal, and he heard you. He has lifted us from the bonds of slavery to a nation set apart for him, and he will not abandon us...his people. By his promise we will not be destroyed. People of Rayl...on this day, Sovereign Ell Yon will avenge us!"

Raviel raised a mighty fist into the air and the Protector exploded forth a burst of brilliant blue energy into the night sky for all Rayleans to see. The people erupted in deafening cheers and cries for battle.

She looked back toward the off-world pilots, but they were gone.

The commanders began issuing orders to marshal the troops and assault vehicles. General Hart escorted Raviel to the *Ardent*, a destroyer class ground assault craft. It was the best warship the Rayleans had among this rag-tag assault force that had assembled. Soon they would be off, racing to the Shikon River where legions of veteran Kaynian combatants and their advanced vessels of war waited. A single moment of fear swept through Raviel. What of the delta missiles? Raviel realized that she might descend from hero to villain in a day if the outcome were not what she had promised. An image of hundreds of thousands of Rayleans disintegrating at the hand of the Kaynian missiles flashed before her mind. Would the Protector stop them? Could the Protector stop them?

Daeson, Tig, Kyrah, and Rivet made their way to their Starcrafts. They had been refueled and readied by the mechtechs. As they arrived, Lil was waiting for them, her hands noticeably empty.

"I couldn't bring it to you, not without my father knowing," she said apologetically.

"It's okay," Daeson said. "Ell Yon will be with us no matter what. You did the right thing."

"I tried but I couldn't, so instead I brought him." Lil turned.

Chieftain Panodin stepped out from behind a nearby refueling craft and walked toward them. He was carrying a sleek sliver case. The man came to Daeson, eyeing him closely. After a moment his countenance softened.

"These are desperate times," he began. "The very existence of our people hangs in the balance." He glanced toward Lil. "I've been humbled by the faith of my daughter once already. I dare not ignore her now, not when there's so much at stake."

Lil offered a sheepish smile as Panodin continued. "She firmly believes that you are a Navi from Sovereign Ell Yon. The urgency of this battle is pushing me to violate every oath as the Keeper of the Protector I've sworn to uphold. And yet..." Panodin lifted the case to his chest, embracing the jewel of the galaxy. "And yet I must." He looked at Daeson, torn between his duty as Keeper of the Protector and the need to equip a man with the ultimate weapon that could win the day...a man who was a complete stranger.

Daeson looked at the struggling man. "Chieftain Panodin, there's nothing I could say in this moment to convince you of our honest intentions or of my service to Ell Yon as a Navi. Our time is up, and you must choose."

Panodin grimaced. Tig fidgeted next to Daeson. Fighters around them began spooling up their engines.

"Father. You've done well in its keeping. It's time to trust them," Lil said, placing a hand on his arm. She reached for the case and Panodin let her take it. She held it out before her father. He took a deep breath then entered the code that opened the top of the case in multiple directions. The Protector was already resonating with ribbons of blue energy...anticipatory. It alarmed Panodin. He cautiously reached in and lifted it out of the case, wisps of blue dancing across his hands and arms.

"You've done the right thing," Daeson said. He took the Protector and pushed it onto his right forearm. Daeson closed his eyes as the synaptic connection took hold. He submitted, took a deep breath then opened his eyes to see Lil and Panodin staring at him with wonder in their eyes. Daeson's eyes gleamed with the presence of Ell Yon resounding through his body. Lil smiled.

"See father...see his eyes! A second Navi is here to fight with us!"

Panodin's shoulders sunk with relief.

"Time to roll," Tig said as he and Kyrah turned to climb into their Starcraft.

Daeson looked at Lil and Panodin. "This must be our secret. The first Navi that came to you has rallied the people, and they trust her. This must not change. No one knows...agreed?"

Panodin and his daughter nodded. Daeson looked at Lil. "You have a noble heart. Dreams are the stuff of hope and adventure."

Lil's smile spread clear across her face.

"It's time, my liege," Rivet said. "The rendezvous is in fourteen point three minutes, and we can't be late."

Raviel stood on the forward deck of the *Ardent*, Chieftain Luas and General Hart beside her. The *Ardent* was a ground assault striker class destroyer armed with eight high intensity concussion missile launchers, twelve class 2 plasma cannons, four class 4 plasma canons, two matrix burst laser guns, and two subsonic disrupters. It was a serious war fighting machine in and of its own right, but it was no match for the many larger drakken-class destroyers the Kaynians had.

Raviel searched the dark misty horizon beyond the Shikon River. In this season, the Shikon River was at its lowest elevation. Just a few feet deep and only forty feet across on average, it was crossable up and down its entire length. Raviel scanned down their line of forces, seeing the flash of lights of innumerable combatants for as far as she could see in both directions. Up in the sky behind her, the view unobstructed despite the rising mist of the river, she could see the sparkle of thousands of crafts marshalling. Although Raylean sensors had given them some indication of the strength of enemy forces, the electronic spoofing and visual cloaking technology employed by the Kaynians made a precise assessment impossible. The dark of night was just now giving way to the dawning day. Pink, orange and blue hues streaked off the underside of cirrus clouds as the morning light pushed the world of Rayl into a battle of the ages. It was horrific to think that the beauty of the day would soon be bludgeoned with the blood of thousands, perhaps hundreds of thousands.

Dawn fully broke, and Raviel began to see just what they were facing. One-half a mile across the river, on conquered Raylean soil was a massive army of supreme power. And up above them hovered thousands of elite war craft, all carrying the deadly delta missiles. Raviel could now clearly see their own lines extending up and down the river for as far as the eye could see. Two massive military forces in a standoff, each one waiting for the other to flinch. This wasn't the usual way of modern warfare, but the natural boundary of the Shikon River along with the escalating political and military build-up had forced this archaic standoff upon them both.

Every Raylean soldier now turned their eyes to Raviel. As she gazed across the expanse and knew that millions of fellow Rayleans were being enslaved and oppressed in their own lands by this ruthless enemy, the fury of a vengeful Immortal began to fill her heart.

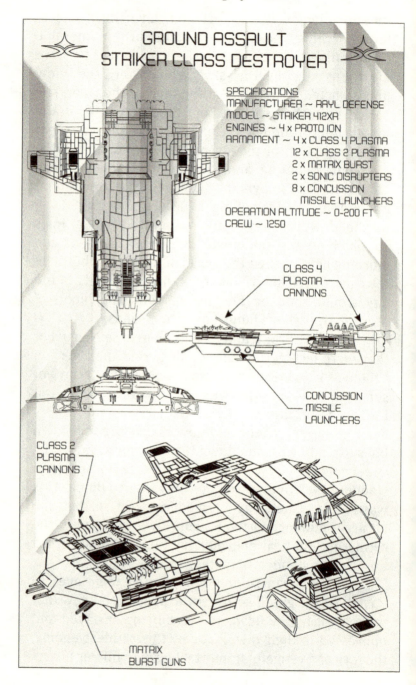

GROUND ASSAULT
STRIKER CLASS DESTROYER

SPECIFICATIONS
MANUFACTURER ~ RAYL DEFENSE
MODEL ~ STRIKER 412XR
ENGINES ~ 4 x PROTO ION
ARMAMENT ~ 4 x CLASS 4 PLASMA
            12 x CLASS 2 PLASMA
            2 x MATRIX BURST
            2 x SONIC DISRUPTERS
            8 x CONCUSSION
                MISSILE LAUNCHERS
OPERATION ALTITUDE ~ 0-200 FT
CREW ~ 1250

CLASS 4
PLASMA
CANNONS

CONCUSSION
MISSILE
LAUNCHERS

CLASS 2
PLASMA
CANNONS

MATRIX
BURST GUNS

General Sisero was waiting...waiting to see if the rumors of a Raylean Navi were true...waiting to see if they would turn and run from their indomitable might.

At the appointed moment, Raviel lifted her hand high into the air for all the world to see. She felt the deck of the *Ardent* buzz with energy as its mighty weapons powered up. It was time for battle, but before she could drop her arm to mobilize their force of 500,000 combatants, the sky above the Kaynian forces lit up with thousands of bright orange streaks. The Kaynian aero craft had launched. Two seconds later, the roar of 1,400 delta missiles assaulted their ears with the sound of imminent death. The soldiers of Rayl did not run, nor did they cry out in fear. They looked upward and watched in silence, knowing that within seconds more than half of them would probably all be dead. "Navi," Luas said at her right side. "We must get you below deck. There's a good chance you'll survive so you can lead the survivors into battle."

Raviel clenched her fist, waiting. Her stomach churned as the Protector remained silent and still.

"No," she said over her shoulder. "I belong here."

Sovereign Ell Yon...where are you? she pleaded.

Suddenly, over a thousand targeting laser beams appeared, emanating from the distant Kaynian aero craft. The beams were focused on all of the destroyers, frigates, and at perfectly spread intervals across the ground forces up and down the Shikon River. There seemed no hope of surviving this rain of death. Then, a glint of white caught Raviel's eye as the two off-world Starcraft broke from the Raylean aerotech formation above them. The roar of the Starcraft engines joined the sound of precipitous doom. Screaming downward toward their own ground forces, Raviel wondered if this was the work of the Kaynians, a preemptive strike from traitors that had been purchased to attack their own people. Raviel fumed...she had been right to suspect them. But just as the two craft were reaching weapons range, they banked sharply to the right in perfect formation, flying just overhead parallel to the river. An instant later, the Protector on Raviel's arm exploded in a blinding burst of power, the likes of which the world had never seen. The Kaynian delta missiles were now midway to their targets, descending on the soldiers of Rayl, but that was about to change. The Protector's ribbon of Immortal blue energy hit one of the off-world Starcraft and then instantly dispersed in 1400 different paths of laser-like beams of energy right back at the aero craft that had launched them.

"The targeting lasers of the Kaynians are gone!" exclaimed General Hart. Not a single beam of light remained on any of the Raylean forces.

"And look!" Chieftain Luas shouted, pointing up at the delta missiles.

The trajectory of all 1400 delta missiles had pitched sharply downward, reversing direction and were now flying back across the river.

"The Protector has overridden their targeting lasers," Hart declared.

Three seconds later, the far side of the river erupted in a cacophony of thunderous explosions that made the ground beneath them shudder. The distant sound of screaming Kaynian soldiers filled the air as they endured the plight of their own destruction.

"Now!" Raviel ordered, dropping her hand to signal the attack. The shouts of 500,000 voices lifted to the skies as the entire ground seemed to move forward and across the river. Above them, the off-world Starcraft barrel-rolled then pitched up vertically, signaling to all of the other aerotech craft to advance.

The skies above turned into a wild mesh of plasma and laser fire that nearly outshone the morning rays of the sun. Within the first few minutes, it became evident that the Kaynian forces were in complete and utter panic. They attempted a retreat, but the Rayleans would not have it, for the Kaynians had occupied Raylean ground, imprisoning Raylean citizens. The forces of the Navi advanced on the Kaynians with fierceness, leaving no quarter for the army of General Sisero. Raviel led the charge in the *Ardent* along with ground assault destroyers, frigates, and troop carriers, pursuing and destroying enemy ground forces in each city, town and village while the Raylean aerotech forces above demolished every single airborne craft the Kaynians had sent. The campaign to retake their nation lasted for two grueling days until they reached the sea.

Near the coastal city of Cargal, 5,000 Kaynians gathered to make a final stand. General Hart ordered his 400 marines aboard the *Ardent* to deploy in an effort to quell this resilient force. Much to Chieftain Luas's chagrin, Raviel led the charge along with another 6,000 Rayleans from multiple troop carriers. The ground fighting was intense, but since the Rayleans ruled the skies, multiple fighters provided cover and close air support when the battle became desperate. At one point, Raviel was pinned down with nine other marines, taking heavy fire from a class two mobile plasma cannon. She called for reinforcements, but before they arrived, one of the off-world Starcrafts appeared out of nowhere and decimated the cannon with precision.

"That thing seems to be everywhere," shouted one of her accompanying marines.

"At least everywhere you are, Navi," added another.

Raviel glowered, looking at the smoldering site that just seconds earlier was raining fierce plasma fire on them. "Let's move!" she ordered, taking a quick glance up at the Starcraft as it banked hard to the left then pitched up to reposition.

Once they regained the city of Cargal, Raviel ordered them to advance across the isthmus onto the continent of the Kaynians, pursuing General Sisero clear to the Kaynian capitol city of Bolshick. Here, with most of the Kaynian elite forces destroyed, they quickly defeated and conquered the remaining enemy forces, restoring freedom to their brothers and sisters that had been enslaved there. General Sisero and Prefect Binja were captured and brought before the Navi for judgment.

In the court of their esteemed city, Raviel and her generals confronted Sisero and Binja, two evil men that had inflicted decades of sorrow and death on the Raylean people.

"What is your judgment?" Chieftain Luas asked.

Raviel examined the men, seeing their loathing hate for her and for her people in their eyes.

"Their lives are not for me to judge, but for Sovereign Ell Yon," Raviel replied. "He will decide their fate."

Raviel looked to the Raylean soldiers holding Sisero and Binja. "Stand away," she ordered. The men stepped aside as Raviel lifted the Protector and spread her hand wide.

The smug countenances of the two men instantly vanished as the Protector expelled a piercing flame of energy. For one brief moment their faces illumined in the judging power of the Immortal, then they both vanished away leaving only remnant ashes which slowly settled to the marble floor. There were gasps from the remaining leaders of the Kaynians, but the Raylean victors said nothing.

Raviel looked toward Chieftain Luas and General Hart. "We're done here," she said, then turned and walked away, leading her people back home...back to Rayl.

CHAPTER

8

The Victory Gala

Daeson carefully approached the head table where Raviel was seated joyfully celebrating the victory with the chieftains and the forcetech and aerotech commanders. The music and the festivities continued behind him, but Raviel and her companions ceased their conversations, watching as Daeson approached. Chieftain Luas stood and walked to Daeson with a fierce look in his eyes. Daeson broke his gaze from Raviel and addressed Luas, readying himself for admonishment for his earlier disrespect. Luas lifted his chin slightly.

"You were true to your word, off-worlder. I don't know what happened up there, but it seems Ell Yon has favored you...and so do we. We owe you a debt of gratitude." Luas's hard stare softened as he smiled, offering Daeson his arm. "You and your companions are welcome among us."

As Daeson took his arm, Luas's smile disappeared. His eyes opened wide as he felt the Protector beneath Daeson's sleeve. Daeson lifted a finger to his mouth. "Ell Yon is everywhere," he offered.

Luas's smile returned broader than before. He turned, opening his arm to the head table.

"Please join us and tell us how we can return the favor to you."

"Here, here!" shouted nearly all at the table...all except Raviel. Her eyes were laced with skepticism.

"Thank you, Chieftain Luas, and the gallant leaders of this great nation. I and my companions require nothing in return for our service to the people of the great and mighty Sovereign Ell Yon. However, if you might allow me to be so bold as to ask one small favor?"

Luas looked to Raviel who sat silently watching the exchange. She offered one subtle nod. Luas smiled his approval.

"What is your request?" he asked.

Daeson fixed his eyes on Raviel. "I would be most honored if the Navi would bestow upon me a single dance."

Luas and all of those seated at the table became silent. The rest of the hall seemed to notice the apprehension of the moment. The music faded as thousands turned their attention to the head table. All eyes fell on Raviel. For the first time since seeing her in this time, Daeson saw her resolve falter. Daeson and every occupant in the large hall waited for her response.

The battle was over, the victory won. The hearts of the Raylean people had returned to Sovereign Ell Yon, and Raviel was content...almost. She had come to believe that she would continue to fulfill the role the people of Rayl needed as their Navi. Her purpose seemed so sure. But in her contentment was one small shadow of doubt. It first appeared with the off-world pilots...well, one of them. When he approached the table, her heart began to race, and she didn't understand why. Was it simply that he was an unsolved mystery? There was a corner of her mind, and her heart, where she dared not venture. Now, he had come to force her to look there, and it angered her. Whereas before she had desperately searched for her past, she now had come to fear it, or rather how it might change her significant purpose as the Navi, and yet Ell Yon had clearly used this man as some strange conduit of the Protector's power.

Thousands were looking on. Certainly, the nation of Rayl owed this man and his companions their appreciation, but his request was humiliating... offensive. Surely the Navi of Ell Yon should not dance before the eyes of the nation. She glanced at the man, then to Luas, then to the thousands that looked on. He had cornered her, and it made her furious. She would not be made a spectacle of! Besides this, she wasn't even sure she knew how to dance. She opened her lips to deny, but the man closed the distance to the table and bowed.

"I would be honored, my Navi. Please."

Raviel's eyes narrowed, despising the situation this man was forcing upon her, but she stood, walked around the table and came to stand before him.

"One," she said sternly, steeling her heart against the emotions that seemed to linger in the shadows.

The man offered a gentle smile, holding up his arm for her to take. She placed her left hand on his raised forearm and shivers flitted up and down her spine as her fingers felt the stiff form beneath his sleeve. She looked up at him, astonished. Was this...a Protector? Her heart skipped a beat as her own Protector seemed to resonate with affirming power. She locked her gaze on him, her mind filling with a hundred questions. The man only offered a quick side glance her way as he led them to the center of the dance floor. The crowd parted, watching with great anticipation. The man turned, bowed, and stepped back to allow the dance to begin. Raviel bowed her head appropriately, and the music began.

Raviel trusted her subconscious memory and her muscles to guide her, and it worked. She moved her body to synchronize with his movements, finding it surprisingly easy to do so. As the dance commenced, everyone else looked on, somehow knowing that this dance was theirs and theirs alone. Raviel turned in perfect motion, fulfilling the movements of the timeless Raylean tradition. Her heart began to race as the crescendo of the dance arrived to the moment of the touch. She and the man closed their distance to within one pace where she then lifted and rotated the back of her hand to his. He gently pushed the back of his hand against hers. The innocent contact sent a shockwave of powerful feelings throughout her body, and she nearly faltered because of it. Who was this man that affected her so? After one full circle, the backs of their hands separated, and she was thankful, although she could not separate from his gaze. He continued to peer into her soul, threatening to expose the shadows of her mind. A moment later, the backs of their hands touched once more, and it was too much for Raviel. Something flashed clear through her mind...a tidal wave of knowing. It lasted but a microsecond, but it undid her. He was closer than before, just inches away from her. She nearly pulled away, wanting to run and hide. Her gaze went to the thousands of her people looking on all around them.

"Who are you," she whispered, steeling herself.

The man's penetrating eyes softened to a glow of warmth. He opened his lips to answer, but the dance separated them once more, forcing another sixty seconds of confused contemplation. Three more movements and the dance would be over. She just had to last another minute. The final notes of the music rushed in on her, and the two of them closed to within a few inches once more. She wanted and rejected what was happening all at the same time. The man lifted his hand for the final touch, turning his palm to her hand. She lifted the back of her hand to his and the people of the hall held their breath, sensing something intensely personal was happening before their eyes. Would she turn her hand...would she welcome him?

Raviel gazed into his eyes, his face just inches from hers. Emotions and memories threatened to crush her, and she didn't know whether to welcome them or hide from them. Raviel couldn't...she did not turn her hand, rejecting the intimacy of his final touch. His eyes filled with pain. She didn't want to know who he was for it would undo everything she had won here. She dropped her hand and walked away, feeling the gaze of the man and a thousand silent spectators pushing on her. She would not go back to the head table...she would run from this place...from him!

"Raviel!"

The man's voice pierced her mind with a name that shattered her resolve. She stopped fifteen paces away from him, frozen. Her head dropped as memories threatened to awaken her past.

"You know me, Raviel," he called out.

Raviel slowly turned around. The man was beckoning with his voice...with his heart. A fellow wearer of the Protector...a fellow Navi. She looked into his eyes, daring for one brief moment to peer into the shadow of her mind.

Raviel! the quiet voice of Ell Yon affirmed. A pulse of healing power flowed from the Protector, unlocking the doors of her mind. As if the curtains of a dark room had been thrown open, the enormity of her past rushed in, and Raviel remembered. The man before her opened his arms, pleading. Her eyes lit with the full knowledge of all that she was and also had become. Tears filled her eyes as she embraced her true self once more.

"Daeson," she whispered.

Daeson nodded, tears of his own spilling down his cheeks. "It's me, Rav."

"Daeson!"

Raviel began to walk back to him, then ran. The dance was not over as she threw herself into his embrace. Daeson lifted her up and spun around, a finale to the dance of their lives. Raviel buried her face into his neck and wept.

"You came for me! Again...you came for me."

"I always will, my love," Daeson said.

The audience of the hall erupted in applause and cheerful shouts of acclamation. Soon Tig, Kyrah, and Rivet joined them in the center of the hall. Raviel embraced each one in turn, humbled by the selfless loyalty of their actions.

The celebration of the victory at Shikon River continued late into the night. Lil joined them, anxious to hear of the spectacular stories of her heroes. As the hours passed, Raviel discovered that she was facing the oddest of challenges...how to merge her two selves back into one person. However long that took, she knew that her duty to the Raylean people wasn't over as their Navi. But now she had Daeson, Tig, Kyrah and Rivet to help her. Finally, the world felt right.

There was an enormous amount of work to be done. In the months that followed, Raviel, serving as Navi, along with Daeson, Tig, and Kyrah worked tirelessly to rebuild the nation of Rayl, often performing as diplomats between the splintered clans and their people. After nearly a year had passed, much healing and restoration had been accomplished, and the Rayleans had reestablished themselves as a dominant world power on the planet. Many of the tech orders had begun the process of revitalization, especially the aerotech, forcetech, and scitech orders. Daeson even orchestrated a retrieval mission of the omegeon canisters from the collectors positioned near the Omega Nebula since the sensors indicated they had reached full capacity. The scitechs immediately began the lengthy process of building a third Protector.

With the Rayl recovery fully accelerated, Raviel and her team began to face their real challenges. There were many days of frustration as they negotiated tenuous relations between clans and clan chieftains that often escalated into severe conflicts. When Daeson, Tig, and Kyrah were at their wits' end in such situations, Raviel seemed to be the only leader that could resolve and mitigate the tension.

"Were it not for you, Rav, I think these clans would take up arms against each other," Daeson said one evening as the four of them rejoined for a rare evening meal together.

"Agreed," Kyrah added. "That and the fact that we're surrounded by enemies on all sides."

Raviel was frustrated too. "I have to admit...it *is* a bit discouraging." She glanced at her three dinner mates. "Seems that mutual tragedy is the only thing that keeps them together." She looked over at Daeson. "Is this really what Ell Yon intended for his people? To bicker and fight with each other when some enemy isn't threatening to exterminate them?"

Daeson shook his head. "No, I'm quite certain this isn't what he had in mind. We must remember that these people are free agents. As a leader goes, so goes the nation. We must continue to show them the way...to teach them of Sovereign Ell Yon."

Raviel's heart grew heavy. "And what if we're not here to do that?"

Daeson, Tig, and Kyrah became silent. They all knew what Raviel was referring to. It was a constant burden on the hearts of each of them. Daeson reached for Raviel's hand.

"Is something happening?" Daeson asked.

Raviel's gaze dropped to her plate. "I don't know. There was a moment last week when it felt like I was slipping." She looked up and saw the sober concern on their faces. "I'm sorry," she whispered.

Kyrah stood up from her place at the table and came to Raviel. She bent over and hugged her from behind.

"It's okay, Raviel," Tig said, reaching for her arm. "We're here for you. Wherever you go, we go."

Raviel hung on to Kyrah's arms. How could she possibly repay such selfless acts of love? Words could not convey the depth of gratitude she felt. She humbly retreated into their relentless support.

"I lost my memory for a time," she said biting her lip. "What if something worse happens next time...what if I never remember who you are?"

Daeson squeezed her hand. "Let's not concern ourselves with something that hasn't happened. Ell Yon is with you and with us wherever and whenever we are."

Raviel nodded.

"We must prepare the leadership," Daeson continued. "And you mustn't fly anymore. If a time slip event occurs, we need to be able to recover you safely."

Raviel thought for a moment. "All right."

Kyrah squeezed Raviel once more. "One day this will all be over," she said, then sat down beside Tig.

Daeson looked at their two courageous and loyal friends. His heart swelled as he thought of what they were sacrificing for Raviel and him.

"When this is over, what will you two do?" he asked.

Tig and Kyrah exchanged glances and smiles with each other. Kyrah leaned against Tig's shoulder while reaching for his hand to hold.

"Well," Tig began, "we've tried extreme adventure, and we're thinking we'd like to find a quaint country home and give peace and quiet a turn."

Kyrah's eyes sparkled as Tig shared their dream.

"That sounds absolutely sublime," Raviel said with a sigh.

It was then that Daeson purposed in his heart to make their dream a reality. They had given so much and asked for nothing in return. He swore an oath to himself to make it so.

Two weeks later at the next Council of Chieftains, Raviel addressed the leadership. She stepped into the inner circle. Now every table was occupied. She glanced around the room, seeing the deep respect that each chieftain held for her. This wouldn't be easy.

"My time as your Navi is coming to an end."

There was an audible swell of astonishment.

"No, Navi," Luas objected. "You must stay with us. There's so much yet to accomplish for you."

Raviel looked to the man. Over the past year, he had become a friend and a confidant, and she had grown to genuinely like the man.

"My departure is something that I can't control," Raviel offered sympathetically. "If I could, I would remain with you. I'm sorry."

Small conversations rose up, and Raviel allowed them. Within minutes there was a clamor that was indicative of the ever-present tension between clans. Panodin stood and was finally able to bring order back to the council.

"If your departure is imminent," Panodin stated, "then you must appoint a new leader or else we will splinter again and be vulnerable to our enemies."

"Yes!" shouted several other chieftains. "Appoint a prefect to lead us!"

This seemed to energize the entire council as they considered the prospect of having a leader like the rest of the nations on Rayl.

"No!" Raviel protested. "Sovereign Ell Yon is your prefect!"

"But we need a leader that walks among us," rebutted the chieftain of the Simak Clan.

Raviel became angry. "You want to be like every other nation? To be ruled by a prefect who will take advantage of you and confiscate your property?"

"If he will protect us from our enemies...yes!" exclaimed one chieftain. Her shouts were soon joined by others. The discord in the room rose sharply in support of the motion for a prefect.

In spite of Raviel's disgust, the Protector countered her emotions.

Give them a prefect, Ell Yon's whisper said clearly.

Raviel thrust her arm into the air, and the room immediately fell silent as the Protector showered the room in a display of blue energy. She walked to Panodin, and the man's countenance filled with fear. Raviel glared down at him, then she slowly lowered her hand until the brilliant light of the Protector encompassed him completely. Panodin cringed, surely thinking his end had come.

"You are not him," Raviel said, then moved to the chieftain of the Jahrim Clan, leaving Panodin alive and grateful. After scanning Chieftain Vansan, Raviel repeated, "You are not him." She continued eliminating each of the Clan leaders until she came to the last chieftain, Luas of the Baraquet Clan. When Raviel lowered the glow of the Protector onto him, the room momentarily filled with the brilliance of the sun, then the light diminished completely. Raviel stared at the man who had once threatened her, then became a close friend.

"You are him," she said quietly. "Prefect Luas, lead your people well."

Reverence filled the room as the other chieftains acknowledged the first prefect of the Raylean people, offering their allegiance to him. Raviel left the room, disheartened by what she'd had to do. Although it was the bidding of Ell Yon, in her heart she knew the Sovereign didn't want this to have happened.

They are a stiff-necked people, the whisper said. *Their folly is not yours.*

In the evening of the following day, Raviel paid a visit to Chieftain Panodin. He invited her to the back terrace where they could look out onto the country with a completely different outlook than when she had first visited here.

"To what do I owe the pleasure of your visit, Navi?" Panodin asked, his eyes conveying a measure of concern.

Raviel continued to gaze at the serene landscape. She then turned and saw the outline of Jalem, feeling the intense need of the people weighing heavily on her shoulders. She would love nothing more than to stay and lead them through the challenging days ahead, but she could feel the impending spacetime anomaly lurking behind each tick of time.

"The people have a prefect to lead them, but they will also need a Navi to guide them...to be the voice of Ell Yon," she said, still gazing across the countryside. She looked down at the Protector, peacefully encompassing her arm. She gently touched it then turned and looked at Panodin.

Panodin's eyes opened wide as his gaze fell to the Protector.

"Navi...I can't. Surely there must be another that is more worthy than I."

"This isn't for you," Raviel said, letting her eyes convey the message to come.

The fear in Panodin's eyes dissipated. "But...," Panodin closed his eyes and smiled. "I see...of course." He looked at Raviel's piercing eyes. "Ell Yon is no respecter of persons...nor of age."

"He looks upon the heart," Raviel said.

"Shall I call her?" Panodin asked.

Raviel nodded.

A couple of minutes later, Lil stepped onto the terrace.

"Raviel!" she exclaimed, running to meet her. Raviel embraced the young woman. She hadn't been able to see Lil much over the course of the last year and was surprised to see how mature Lil had become in just twelve short months.

"It's so good to see you!" Lil was smiling ear to ear. "Can you stay for a while?"

"I'm afraid not."

Lil's joy instantly abated. "But Father said you wanted to see me."

"I do, Lil." Raviel took hold of Lil's hands. "I have something very important to give to you. Although you're young, Ell Yon sees a heart of faithfulness in you that is rare among our people."

Lil glanced to the ground in humility.

"My time here is short," Raviel added.

Lil looked back up at Raviel, her forehead creasing with concern. "No, Navi...we need you...I need you!"

Raviel peered deep into Lil's eyes. "Actually, the people need *you*, Lil." She carefully took hold of the Protector and lifted it from her arm, instantly feeling the void in her soul. "You've been chosen by Sovereign Ell Yon to be the next Navi." She held the Protector in front of Lil.

Lil's mouth opened as she took a step back. "Surely not me!" Her hand went to her chest, stunned by the offer. She glanced toward her father who stood statuesque, watching, proud.

"I'm just nineteen," Lil protested. "Who will listen to me?"

"It's not you they will be listening to," Raviel said. "It won't be easy, and it will alter your life forever...but it will be a life of extreme purpose." Raviel rested a sympathetic hand on Lil's shoulder. "The choice is yours."

Lil gazed back into Raviel's eyes, took a deep breath and held out her arm. Raviel nodded. Such a good heart, and one of such courage and humility. Ell Yon always surprises with such profound wisdom. Raviel placed the Protector above Lil's arm and pushed the solid vambrace downward. It molded itself to the form of the young woman. Lil closed her eyes tightly as the synaptic interface completed. Seconds later she opened her eyes, and Lil saw the edges of the galaxy there. The transformation from girl to Navi was remarkable.

"Come with me, my young Navi," Raviel said. She took Lil to the Navi Hall of Meditation, the place where they had first met. For the next two hours, Raviel offered Lil counsel in regard to the Protector and to the people. Being a Navi in conjunction with a prefect was new ground. Perhaps this was what the people really needed after all. Raviel was hopeful that the time of their wandering hearts would come to an end. Perhaps now they would remain the people of Ell Yon forever.

With Lil beside her, Raviel looked out from the hillside and onto the city of Jalem. Lil looked over at her mentor. "All of a sudden the galaxy seems a thousand times bigger than it used to be. I'm a little overwhelmed."

Raviel opened her mouth to speak, but the world shifted, then settled into place.

"When times are hard, remember that Ell Yon makes no mistakes."

"Are you okay, Raviel?" Lil asked.

"Tell Daeson," Raviel said, then vanished.

CHAPTER

5

Judgment

aviel was desperate to keep a hold on her mind, fearing that with each time slip, a little more of her would dissolve away. If she lost her memories again, would she ever find them? Although she still felt the molecular-level decay of her being, on this journey through time her mind seemed to stay anchored. Without the Protector, she felt particularly vulnerable, and yet somehow, Ell Yon was still with her. Remarkably, her mind began to fill with a collage of scenes, glimpses of what was happening to the Rayleans as she slipped past. Watching key events unfold before her eyes angered her. In spite of her anger, there was also a sense of excitement and reborn hope that accompanied the frustration for what she saw. When the world formed once again around her, she was still whole, her mind and memories intact. Lil was gone, but the Navi Hall of Meditation didn't seem to have changed much. Raviel knelt down, taking a moment to recover. If what Sovereign Ell Yon had shown her was the extent of the time slip, just decades, not centuries, had passed. She stood, considering her next actions, the flame of anger still flickering in her eyes. She went to the alcove that Daeson had previously arranged and placed her hand on the bio panel. A section of the wall slid silently away and she gasped.

"Oh Daeson!"

At the bottom of the alcove was a Protector...silent, waiting. Was it functional, she wondered? She carefully lifted the treasured vambrace from its resting place. Reverently, she pushed the Protector onto her right forearm. Any question as to its authenticity was immediately dispelled, for the mind of Ell Yon flooded her thoughts with affirming judgment. Raviel took a moment to absorb the Immortal's call then went to the pillars that allowed her to look out onto the grand city of Jalem. She inhaled the crisp cool fall air of the country, then made straightaway for the palace that was occupied by the leader of Rayl, Prefect Luas. As her thoughts turned to the man she had called a friend, she struggled in her heart. Across five decades of time Ell Yon had revealed a vivid portrayal of Luas's actions as prefect and Raviel sorrowed, for the man had allowed the position of power to ruin him. Thoughts of Daeson, Tig, Kyrah, and Rivet vied for her attention, but she concluded that they were either here already or would be soon so she instead focused on the mission set before her.

Once she reached the Palace, guards tried to detain her, but she would have none of it. Multiple bursts of Protector power quickly put the entire palace in a state of pandemonium as Raviel arrived at two massive doors, the only remaining protection for a prefect petrified of a Navi with a message and a mission. Raviel burst into the room and marched straight up to stand before an aged Prefect Luas. Counselors, generals, and palace guards waited, nervously fingering their weapons yet not willing to invite calamity.

Prefect Luas's eyes opened wide once he realized who Raviel was.

"Impossible!" he exclaimed.

Raviel raised her right hand to the cowering form of Luas. She then closed each finger until only her index was left outstretched, pointing condemnation toward the man, all while wisps of blue energy pulsed from the jeweled ribbons of the Protector.

"You have despised the commands of Ell Yon. You have shunned the Navi Ell Yon sent to guide you. Your arrogance will be the end of you and of your rule in Rayl."

Luas cowered at her condemning words, yet Raviel could see the prideful look of determined insolence lingering in his eyes. He feared only for what Ell Yon might do to him in the moment. There was no remorse for the selfish acts that power, prestige, and privilege had planted in his heart.

"You bestowed the position of prefect on me," Luas countered, attempting to gather courage to stand against this Navi ghost from his past. "I ruled as was necessary to keep Rayl safe."

"You ruled with selfish pleasure," Raviel retorted. "And because of this, another has been chosen and will rule in your place. One who is meek and lowly in heart. His dominion will forever be esteemed and yours despised. By him shall the lineage of reclamation be established."

Luas lifted his chin in prideful defiance, and Raviel's heart broke.

"I called you friend." She shook her head, mourning for the state of the man. "These are the words of Ell Yon. It shall be accomplished."

Luas stiffened, waiting for the final judgment of the Immortal to whom the nation of Rayl belonged, but no immediate judgment came. Raviel lowered her arm, then turned and left, the entire court of the palace watching with great apprehension as she passed by. She had the unexpected notion that her mission here was already complete. The Protector led her out of the city and to a small country home nestled at the foot of the hills beneath the Navi Hall of Meditation. Carefully manicured hedges and a well-kept garden were evidence of the ordered ways of its occupant. Raviel stepped up onto a covered terrace decorated quaintly with carefully chosen artistic pieces. She walked to the entrance and knocked softly on the door, but no one answered. She left the terrace, walking around the home and through a vine covered gate which stood as guardian to a beautiful flower garden. Near the back, Raviel could see the bent form of the garden's tenant.

"Hello?" Raviel called out so as not to startle the person. Her beckon seemed to fall on deaf ears.

Raviel walked through the garden, being careful with her approach.

"Hello," she called again, now just a few paces from the bent form who was working diligently to plant a tray of vibrant flowers Raviel had never seen before.

"I have nothing you want. Leave me alone," the elderly woman said, not tarrying from her labor.

"I seek the Navi of Rayl," Raviel said. The woman paused for just a moment but did not look up.

"Rayl doesn't seem to think it needs a Navi anymore. Be on your way," the woman replied, then resumed her work.

Raviel stepped closer, kneeling down beside the woman. She placed a gentle hand on her arm.

Quietly, she spoke to the woman. "Lil...it's me, Raviel."

Lil froze, then slowly turned her head, all at once capturing Raviel's gaze. Her eyes immediately filled with tears. Decades of lonely, unrequited passion for the people of Rayl spilled out of her eyes and onto the soil of her work.

"Raviel," she whispered. "Is it really you?"

Raviel nodded, leaning toward her. Lil turned, lifting herself up to embrace her friend from another life. The two Navi held on in a knowing that only they could share.

"All the world has left the ways of Ell Yon," Lil said with a heavy heart. "I've tried." Lil's arms weakened. "I've tried."

Raviel squeezed all the more. "The life of a Navi is hard, lonely, and difficult," Raviel responded. She released Lil so she could see her face again. Lil wiped the tears away from her cheeks with soiled hands. "But don't lose hope, my dear friend. Ell Yon is still here...still for us...still for Rayl."

Raviel stood lifting Lil with her. She guided her to a stone bench just a few feet away. They sat then turned toward each other. Lil lifted a hand to Raviel's cheek.

"You're still so young and beautiful, just as I remember you."

Raviel smiled. "Ell Yon showed me your work as Navi for the people. You've done well, Lil. These years have been difficult, and yet you persevered and stayed true."

Lil's hand and gaze dropped. She slowly shook her head.

"There seems no hope...to watch the people continually drift away and be enticed by Deitum Prime. How can we possibly survive the forces of Lord Dracus and his minions when the people are so fickle and easily swayed?"

Raviel stayed quiet. She gently touched Lil's right arm where the Protector silently waited beneath her loose-fitting sleeve. Lil covered Raviel's hand with her own.

"I know," Raviel said. "At times I wish I didn't hear his voice. At other times he doesn't speak. It's hard feeling responsible for the paths of the people when no one will listen."

A fierce look filled Lil's eyes. "Prefect Luas has lost his way."

"That's why I've come," Raviel said. "Ell Yon has judged him."

Lil looked discouraged. She pulled back her sleeve and reached for the Protector, intent on pulling it from her arm.

"Then my time has come," she said sadly.

Raviel reached out and stopped her. "No, my friend. Your time is at hand. You must choose the next prefect. One who will lead the people back to Ell Yon."

Lil looked at Raviel with eyes empty of hope. "It's been a long time since I've heard the voice of Ell Yon. At times it's hard not to think we've been abandoned because of the foolish actions of the prefect and his leaders." Her gaze dropped to the ground. "It's hard not to despair for the future of Rayl. I do wonder what you'll find when you arrive there."

Raviel felt Lil's despondency in a very real way, often wondering the same things herself. She grabbed Lil's hand.

"Lil, I've learned to put my faith in Ell Yon, not in the actions of our people or our leaders. They will always disappoint. You must remember that I've also seen Ell Yon pluck us up from the mire of slavery in Jypton in the most miraculous way and bring us to the promised world of Rayl. His promises are sure, they never expire, and he's not done promising a future, not only to us but to the entire galaxy. I don't know what that looks like, but in some way, your involvement here and now is a key part of that happening."

Lil's eyes filled with wonder, then illumination. She looked away. Raviel could see the glow of the Immortal fill Lil's countenance as the voice of Ell Yon whispered to her mind.

"But he's just a lad," Lil said, turning to look back at Raviel.

"Ell Yon looks upon the heart and not on the stature of a man. It will be your challenge to navigate the transfer of power as you watchguard the lad in the meantime."

Lil's eyes filled with purpose. "And what happens to you now?"

Raviel shook her head. "I wish I knew. I just know that this is your time and not mine." She felt the tremor in her being. She pulled away from Lil.

"Will I see you again?" Lil asked, the creases near her eyes deepening.

"This is it," Raviel said. "I don't know when I will next appear, but it will not be with you."

Lil tried to smile. "Farewell—"

And then the world melted away.

Daeson was confused. Having learned from Raviel's last spacetime anomaly event, he watched the quantum tracker on his wrist carefully. It was his intention to arrive at or before Raviel resolved in the new time. He had previously noticed that the rate of time offset displayed on his receiver began to slow as it approached zero. He had overshot by weeks the first time and was intent on not letting that happen again.

Daeson and Rivet in Viper One Starcraft followed by Tig and Kyrah in Viper Two Starcraft were perfectly synchronized in acceleration and velocity as Daeson monitored the spacetime delta carefully. What confused him was that the receiver indicated that Raviel had abruptly stopped time-slipping. Daeson nearly panicked, realizing that they would overshoot her time unless he acted quickly. He started to initiate shutdown procedures, but then halted as the receiver resumed displaying Raviel's time travel journey.

"What just happened?" Daeson wondered out loud.

"To what are you referring, my liege?" Rivet asked.

"My quantum receiver stalled and then resumed," Daeson replied. "It's almost as if Raviel resolved and then slipped again."

"Unless there is a malfunction with your receiver, that is a logical conclusion."

Daeson swallowed hard. He hadn't considered such a possibility. It meant that Raviel could be anywhere on the planet, unprotected. What if she had time-slipped where a future building was to be constructed? What if she had been traveling, perhaps in space or over an ocean? The potential for tragedy was enormous, especially if her memory had been affected again and she didn't understand her condition. Daeson's heart began to race as he anguished in the moments of uncertainty. His eyes were now fixated on the receiver, watching the months tick by like seconds. Fifteen minutes later it happened. Daeson initiated the shutdown procedure and both Starcraft arrived in orbit around Rayl 420 years after they began their journey. Although the resolution on the quantum receiver wasn't tight enough to know just how early they were, Daeson felt confident that their arrival should be within just a few days of Raviel's. What Daeson didn't expect was a welcoming committee comprised of over 100 warships. The visual was stunning chaos. Massive battleships, frigates, destroyers and hundreds of fighters were descending. The nearest battleship had just launched four additional fighters into the fray. Clearly the planet of Rayl was under siege, and Daeson and his friends had stumbled into the middle of the forces of a powerful armada.

"Unidentified vessel, stand down and prepare to be escorted by Llyonian fighters to a detention dock. You have ten seconds to comply, or you will be destroyed!"

CHAPTER

10

The Empire of Zar

"A prefect shall rise up from Fraytis to accomplish my judgment and will come with ships of great power and speed to deal accordingly and will turn the hearts of Rayl back to me." ~Rimiah, Navi of Ell Yon.

"**W**hat's the call, Viper One?" Tig radioed. Daeson's finger hovered over the Starcraft's arm weapons hot switch. If he armed weapons and engaged, he could probably survive, especially with his cloak tech, but Tig and Kyrah wouldn't. Once they were identified as hostile, this armada would unleash more than a few fighters. Five seconds passed. He closed the protective cover, leaving his weapon systems deactivated.

"Viper Two, stand down. Whatever has happened here, odds are that Raviel is in trouble. We've got to find her in this mess."

"Lead the way," Tig replied.

"Leave weapons cold, and follow me. This won't be easy, but we should have a few minutes before their fighters reach us."

Daeson yanked hard left on the stick, pulling a tight 12 G turn, straining for a few seconds against the forces until the anti-gravity dampeners kicked in. He pitched steep into the atmosphere for a dangerous re-entry vector. Catching a glimpse of Tig and Kyrah following just off his right wing triggered a moment of déjà vu from long ago. Tig's fiery re-entry during a training mission on Jypton was the catalyst that had formed their unbreakable bond of friendship. This would feel similar since they had to throw caution to the wind in an attempt to outrun their pursuers.

"Set E-shields to max and watch your hull temp," Daeson radioed.

Just then two powerful cannon bursts from behind ratcheted the surrounding air with shockwaves. Daeson altered his course every few seconds to thwart a firing solution from the battleship above.

"Four fighters are in pursuit," Rivet said through the mic.

"Copy. Are they within firing range?" Daeson asked.

"I've analyzed their weapon systems," Rivet responded. "Based on the power signature of the craft, we should be able to stay out of range until we fully enter the atmosphere."

"Do you have any idea who we're up against?" Tig interjected.

"I've been monitoring nineteen radio channels from both the Rayleans and the attacking force," Rivet replied. "I've also successfully tapped into the Raylean information network. These ships are from the planet Llyon in the Fraytis System. A powerful prefect known only by the name Zar is ruler of Llyon and apparently one of the most, if not *the* most powerful prefect in the galaxy. He has already conquered eight other systems in this region of the galaxy."

All radios and com went silent as Daeson and Tig processed Rivet's report and also concentrated on their dicey re-entry. It was Kyrah who finally broke the silence.

"Well, that shouldn't be too much to handle," she quipped.

"The Fraytis System is the closest habitable system to Mesos," Daeson added as they finished their re-entry. He leveled off then checked his quantum receiver. It read, "0." Raviel was here.

"I now have a lock on Raviel's location," Rivet reported. "Coordinates have been entered into the navigational computer."

"Viper Two, we're making straight for Raviel's coordinates. Rivet will relay them to you now."

"Are you seeing this, Viper One?" Tig asked.

Daeson looked up from his instruments to see the distant carnage of a ferocious battle. The sun was just breaking the rim of the horizon spotlighting the stage of an epic battle. The Raylean people were launching everything they had in response to the attack by this powerful force. Though valiant, it was a hopeless fight. Their beloved city of Jalem was the focal point of the attack, but it seemed as though nothing could stop the conquest of their entire world by this massive well-armed armada.

"What do we do, Daeson?" Tig asked.

Daeson felt the heart of war forming in his chest as he watched the impending decimation of his people. He yearned to hear the command of Ell Yon but having left the Protector for Raviel in the Navi Hall of Meditation, it would not be. The end of Rayl and his people looked inevitable.

"We find Raviel, then we fight."

"Copy."

Daeson made a beeline for the coordinates flashing on his nav computer. It was not the Hall of Meditation, but rather a rural piece of land in the valley between the Hall and the capitol city of Jalem. Although the four Llyonian fighters were in hot pursuit, they would have enough time to recover Raviel and launch again, provided their timing was perfect. They dropped down and skimmed the terrain to avoid the ensuing battle just a few miles away. Areas of thick morning fog made visual navigation difficult, but Daeson didn't have the luxury of being careful.

Please, Sovereign Ell Yon, protect Raviel, he petitioned.

"Viper Two, fly cover. I'm cloaking and going in to pick her up," Daeson radioed.

"Copy, Viper One."

"Do you still have a lock?" Daeson asked Rivet. "Is she alive?"

"I'm reading two life signs at her coordinates, but I do not yet have a visual."

Daeson deployed his atmospheric air brakes, setting his Starcraft down in just seconds, stirring up waves of mist near a small, abandoned dwelling. Daeson jumped from the cockpit and started his sprint to cover the last hundred yards to Raviel's location.

"Give me updates on the fighters," Daeson radioed Tig as their Starcraft screamed by in a circling pattern overhead.

"Never seen fighters like these...they're fast and maneuverable," Tig radioed. "Be quick."

Daeson drew his Talon and charged it, unsure as to who might be with Raviel. He checked his coordinates as he closed in. The morning fog was dissipating but not fast enough.

"Raviel!" Nothing.

The foliage thickened as he approached. Daeson could make out a shadowy figure that was bent low to the ground. Lying on the ground beneath him was another figure. It had to be Raviel. What was he doing to her?

"Stand up and back away!" Daeson ordered, his finger tightening on his Talon's trigger.

The bent form slowly lifted his head simultaneously dropping a thin hood to his shoulders that had obscured his face. The man was elderly. White hair contrasted the dark garments he wore. Aged eyes full of wisdom peered back through the dewy morning mist. The man's gaze held Daeson for a moment.

"Come," the man beckoned, not rising from his position over Raviel. "She is just now gaining consciousness."

The man didn't appear to be armed. Instead, he was holding a flask of water. Oddly, the ground around Raviel had been completely cleared, void of anything that might have disrupted Raviel's re-emergence from the quantum time slip. Daeson closed the last few paces cautiously until he saw Raviel's face. He rushed in to her.

Daeson holstered his Talon. "Raviel!" he said, reaching for her hand.

Her eyes opened. It had been over 400 years. If her previous time slip had erased her memories, what would her fate be now? He anguished in the moment. Raviel blinked a few times. She looked from Daeson to the elderly man, apparently confused. This distressed

Daeson greatly as he prepared himself for the worst. She tried to speak but no words formed. Daeson carefully lifted her head as the elderly man gave her water to drink. This seemed to instantly revive her, illumination lighting upon her face. She reached for Daeson's neck, pulling him close to her

"Daeson!"

Despite the sound of the ongoing global battle, Daeson's heart erupted with immense joy. Whatever might come, he knew they would face it together. The elderly man backed away, letting their reunion complete.

As Daeson helped Raviel to her feet he looked toward the elderly man. His countenance was heavy with calm sorrow...sorrow reflecting the impending destruction of Rayl.

"Thank you, sir. Who are you?"

"I am Rimiah, Navi of the Rayleans. I am honored to meet the Navi of the Flight from Jypton." His eyes turned to Raviel. "And the Navi of the Conquest of the Kaynians." The man bowed his head.

"Ell Yon led you here?" Daeson asked.

The man nodded. "And to prepare this place for this time. I didn't understand then, but rarely do we understand the ways of the Sovereign."

"Fighters closing fast!" Daeson heard Tig radio through his earpiece just as the sound of a Starcraft's powerful engines split the air above them.

"We must hurry," Daeson said, pulling Raviel with him. "We have a fight to engage in."

"Navi Starlore," Rimiah called out. "Do not engage. This is the judgment of Ell Yon on the Rayleans. They have once again turned aside, rejecting our Sovereign. I warned Prefect Zedeka not to fight against Zar and his armada, but he and the prefect before him have rejected the words of Ell Yon." Rimiah's face turned dark. "Now he will die and many with him. Our world will be taken and our people enslaved." Rimiah held out his arms in a posture of submission. Daeson saw the lower rim of a Protector on his right forearm.

"Do you have Raviel?" Tig radioed. "We're taking fire...need help!"

The sounds of a brutal dogfight filled the skies above. How could he not fight back for Tig...for Kyrah...for all of Rayl? He turned to sprint back to his Starcraft, but Raviel pulled back on his arm.

"No, Daeson. He speaks the truth...all who fight will die." Her eyes were grim. "The Protector showed this to me as I transitioned. We must not fight!"

Daeson turned back to Raviel. "I can't—"

Raviel pulled the Protector from her arm and pushed it on to his. The fierce thoughts of Ell Yon overwhelmed him so completely that he fell to the ground on his knees. He looked up at Rimiah and Raviel, struggling to accept the truth.

"Viper Two...stand down," he radioed to Tig and Kyrah.

"We're hit!" Tig's voice called back. "We're going down!"

"Bail out!" Daeson screamed. He stood and ran to a clearing where he could spot the overhead battle. Smoke and fire were trailing Tig and Kyrah's Starcraft. They were dangerously low.

"Bail out!" he screamed again, but it was too late. Their Starcraft impacted a rocky ridge with a thunderous explosion that shook the ground.

"NO!" Daeson screamed. "No, no, no! We have to get to them," he shouted, reaching for Raviel to return to his Starcraft with him.

"Daeson, they'll just shoot us down too," Raviel said, pulling back on his arm. Her eyes filled with the same pain he was feeling.

Daeson's heart crumbled. He had sworn to be an instrument of a future of peaceful happiness for them—instead he delivered death. And for what? So that the Rayleans could be imprisoned because of their wayward actions once again? Was any of this pain and suffering worth it? Why try to save a people that didn't want to be saved? With Tig and Kyrah gone, the galaxy seemed a lesser place, and it was. Daeson despaired greatly, questioning his very purpose for serving Ell Yon and more so, the people of Rayl.

Two Llyonian fighters flew swiftly to a hover position overhead as an assault craft landed between them and the position of his Starcraft. Daeson and Raviel looked for Rimiah, but he was gone. Moments later five fierce-looking Llyonian marines surrounded them, weapons leveled.

"Cast your weapons to the ground!" their captain ordered.

Daeson carefully tossed his Talon.

"The arm weapon too."

Daeson looked at Raviel. Uncertainty laced her eyes. The Protector had gone silent. Daeson slowly pulled the Immortal tech from his arm and let it fall to the ground. The marines closed in on them, binding their hands behind them.

"Are you the pilots we were pursuing?" the captain demanded.

Daeson hesitated, but one of the marines pressed his plasma rifle up against Raviel's head.

"Yes, we're the pilots," Daeson said quickly.

The captain seemed satisfied. He nodded and the marine pulled back his weapon.

"There were two of you. We destroyed one. Where is the other fighter craft?" the captain pressed.

"My co-pilot was able to escape," Daeson replied hesitantly. He hoped Rivet would know how to handle himself in this unexpected situation, at least keeping the Starcraft cloaked.

The captain's eyes narrowed. "Hmph. We'll find him. We'll rule this entire planet by day's end." He turned to one of his men. "They're fighter pilots. Tag them as P-Ones for the PCM trials."

The marine pulled a small device from his belt pack, tapped a couple of controls then set it against Daeson's shoulder. One more tap and a brief but searing pain accompanied a zapping sound. He placed the device against Raviel's shoulder and repeated the process. The captain pressed a com device on his chest.

"Prisoner transport Baker Baker four seven, two P-Ones for pickup on my coordinates."

He scrutinized Daeson and Raviel for a moment. "You won't survive the trials long but at least it's a better fate than what most of your people will endure." He turned to his men. "Sergeant, prep them for the transport!"

In just a few short minutes, Daeson and Raviel's lives filled with tragedy...unstoppable, painful tragedy. Daeson could hardly bear the thought of Tig's and Kyrah's deaths and the whole of Rayl now either destroyed or enslaved. This was Ell Yon's command? It was a painful truth and overwhelming to consider. He looked to Raviel.

"I'm sorry to have brought you here," she whispered.

Daeson shook his head. "It's not your fault. Our people...will they never learn?"

The battle for Rayl didn't last long. By week's end, the entire planet was under Llyonian control, ruled by Prefect Zar. For Daeson, Raviel, and hundreds of thousands of fellow Rayleans, the journey as prisoners of war back to the homeworld of Llyon was long, painful, and anxious as they endured over seventy-two hours of extreme hunger and thirst. They both were also tormented by thoughts of Tig's and Kyrah's deaths, often sharing sorrowful tears in the remembrance of their loyal trusted friends. And to this sorrow, bitter feelings of national betrayal threatened to overwhelm Daeson and steal away his Navi heart.

CHAPTER

11

Captives

When they finally arrived on Zar's planet, Llyon, Daeson and Raviel were concerned about being split up. Fortunately, that was not the case. A smaller contingent of prisoners designated as P-Ones were all kept together and placed in barrack-style housing. Here they joined hundreds of other pilots that had been captured from other worlds that Zar and his imperial armada had conquered as they spread across this region of the galaxy. Each prisoner was given a numerical designation and addressed as such from that time forward. Daeson was prisoner P-One Delta 381 and Raviel was prisoner P-One Delta 394. Apparently, there were three groups of pilot prisoners that had arrived ahead of them; Alpha, Bravo, and Charlie groups. Information regarding their potential future was slow coming. And although they were treated significantly better than the common prisoners, evidently the lifespan of a P-One prisoner was significantly less than the others. Soon they would find out why.

Even as prisoners of war, Daeson and Raviel could not help but notice the ever-present cocky attitude of their fellow pilots, no matter what world they were from. Something about the world of fighter pilots invited such arrogance. Daeson and Raviel did their best to encourage other Rayleans in their plight despite their own sorrow for the loss of their friends, but it was difficult since they were without the voice of Ell Yon.

Physical examinations were conducted to make sure they were fit. As they were waiting, a fellow prisoner approached them.

"You from Rayl?" he asked Daeson.

"Yes…you?" Daeson returned.

"Not anymore. Raylean prisoners don't fare well here," the man said with a frown. "You know what's going to happen to us?"

"Not at all."

Raviel stepped closer to hear the conversation. The man looked around to see who else might be listening.

"If I were you two, I would do everything you can to fail their tests because those that pass are used for target practice for their war games. We're just plasma fodder. If you wash out, you can at least live as common prisoners. Here…you'll be dead in a matter of months…maybe weeks."

Daeson eyed the man closely. Something about him felt off.

"Mark my words…get out." The man turned and left.

Raviel crossed her arms. "I don't like him."

"Agreed, but it doesn't mean he's not right," Daeson added.

"Perhaps," another voice said from behind them. "But in this case, it does."

Daeson and Raviel turned to see another fighter pilot with the veteran look of many hours of combat in his eyes.

"Banthos is trying to sift out as many P-Ones as possible to increase his odds. He's right about our bleak future but if you wash out, they send you straight to the diconium mines. The Llyonians won't stand for anything less than best efforts, so the consequence of washing out is worse...much worse."

"That I believe," Raviel said. "Thanks."

"No thanks needed. Either way we're in for a tough go of it. No sense making any more enemies than necessary."

"So, what are the PCM trials and the P-Ones all about?" Daeson asked.

"I don't know much, just that PCM stands for Pilot Combat Maneuvering. As far as what the 'trials' are...your guess is as good as mine," the pilot answered. "Zar is intent on building the most formidable empire the galaxy has ever seen. I doubt that what's happening here is just for entertainment. Banthos may be right...there's a military purpose behind it all. The way I see it, prisoners need to stick together, no matter what's in store."

Daeson stuck out his arm.

"I'm Daeson."

"Jaco Ty, from Syroc."

Raviel offered her arm as well.

"Raviel. We're all in this together. Might as well have some friends along the way."

"Copy that," Jaco replied. "Sharing accurate information is a good way to start."

Daeson nodded, then was called in for his physical.

P-One prisoners were expected to keep in top physical condition and participated in a daily exercise regimen. This often afforded both him and Raviel excursions outside to a large court equipped with running tracks and equipment to keep their bodies at peak performance. Llyonian guards were always present, but the elaborate perimeter barriers were more than enough to keep the prisoners from considering a foolish attempt to escape. After all, where would they go? They were on an enemy planet, light years from their homeworlds with no one to turn to for help.

Part of keeping the P-Ones in excellent condition was providing some of the best food and drink Llyon had to offer. However, Daeson and Raviel had purposed in their hearts to abstain from Deitum Prime-laced foods and drinks to remain true to Ell Yon, and so they were careful in this regard.

"Have you ever seen a city so magnificent in all your life?" Raviel asked as she and Daeson ran laps together.

Daeson looked up at the gleaming structures towering above and all around them. Entire sections of the city were levitating at various heights, and the elaborate lush green gardens and parks were simply breathtaking. Exquisite transport crafts of every size were flying in all directions, carrying Llyionians and often their slaves to unimaginable destinations.

"It is truly remarkable," Daeson said. "But in spite of its brilliance, this place has a dark past."

"The AI Wars," Raviel returned.

Daeson nodded. Fables claimed that in addition to Mesos, Llyon was one of the worlds where the androids with artificial intelligence had first rebelled.

"Although I have to admit, in spite of his conquests to garner immense resources and become the most powerful man in the galaxy, Prefect Zar also has an eye for beauty."

Raviel was silent for a time.

"How does Sovereign Ell Yon work through such a powerful man as Zar, endowed by Lord Dracus, to his own cause?"

Daeson glanced over at Raviel. "It's hard to fathom. But he does...somehow he does."

After days of written aptitude tests and a few pilot simulations that tested reaction time and adaptation skills, the number of P-Ones was whittled down significantly. As far as Daeson could tell, there were roughly 200 pilots that remained, he and Raviel being two of them. He continued to teach Raviel every spare moment they had in preparation for whatever they may face. Although their fate was uncertain, he knew one thing for sure...superior skills increased survivability.

The day came for the P-Ones to be divided up and assigned to squadrons, each one led by a veteran Llyonian pilot designated as a captain. All of the P-Ones were escorted to the center of a massive indoor arena equipped with displays, fighter simulation pods, and peripheral control panels that were a mystery to Daeson and Raviel. Eight Llyonian captains and their assistants stood on a circular line surrounding the P-Ones. The captains were equidistant from each other and behind each one was a large display that would soon designate their assigned prisoner trainees. Daeson reached for Raviel's hand and squeezed to help erase some of the lines of worry that were evident on her brow.

"Ell Yon is with us, even now without the Protector."

Raviel nodded, trying to appear confident.

"Prisoner Delta 265 commence to Dagger Squadron under Captain Rolis," a loud voice announced. An image of the prisoner appeared on the large display above one of the captains. The prisoner broke from the others and made his way toward his designated captain.

"Prisoner Delta 381 commence to Thunder Squadron under Captain Ashpen."

Daeson squeezed Raviel's hand once more then let loose and started walking to the two men standing beneath his image. Captain Ashpen looked to be a disciplined, stately and intelligent man who was fifteen years Daeson's senior. The assistant was standing to the captain's side, operating a glass tablet as the drafting of pilots continued. Daeson approached and the captain's eyes narrowed, scrutinizing his new draftee. Daeson surmised that whatever was in store for them, the Llyonian empire had gone through great lengths to identify the best-skilled pilots, and he knew that his performance would reflect on his newly assigned captain's career...perhaps even his livelihood. Daeson stopped a few feet away, bowed his head then looked the man straight in the eye.

"Captain Ashpen, I was trained as a pilot with the Jyptonian Planetary Aero Forces and have extensive combat experience. Prisoner Delta 394 is an equally skilled pilot with combat experience that I have trained for months. You would do well, sir, to draft her into your squadron."

It was a risky move, and Daeson hoped he hadn't jeopardized Raviel's position. It would come down to the character of the man. Captain Ashpen held Daeson's gaze a few more seconds as his assistant quickly tapped and swiped on his tablet.

"Well, Lieutenant Melzar?" Ashpen said without taking his eyes off of Daeson.

"Her scores do meet your standards, sir."

Ashpen hesitated.

"Fall in," he commanded Daeson, then spoke quietly to his lieutenant. A couple of minutes later, the other seven captains had chosen their first picks, and now it would soon be Ashpen's turn to make his second draft. Daeson held his breath.

"Prisoner Delta 394 commence to Thunder Squadron under Captain Ashpen."

Daeson closed his eyes and thanked Ell Yon. Raviel stepped out from the central group of pilots and walked his way. Captain Ashpen turned to look at Daeson.

"If you're wrong about her, I'll kill you both myself."

"I'm not wrong, and you won't regret it," Daeson returned.

Ashpen smirked then prepared for his next draft, but Lt. Melzar offered Daeson a quick reassuring nod. Raviel came and stood quietly beside Daeson, both silently rejoicing.

Once the drafting process was complete and there were no pilots left in the circle, Captain Ashpen turned to address his twenty-five pilot prisoners.

"Listen up, Thunder Squad—"

"Attention all squadron captains," the arena announcer interrupted. "Ten more P-Ones have just arrived and will be assimilated into your units. Standby to submit draft requests."

Ashpen frowned. "I don't need any more. Let the other squadrons have them," he said to Lt. Melzar.

"Yes sir."

Just as Captain Ashpen was about to resume his introductory statement, two guards entered the arena escorting ten more pilots to the center circle. Daeson nearly gasped. He immediately spotted Tig and Kyrah in the group, simultaneously feeling Raviel's hand grip his arm tightly. He nodded.

"I see them," he whispered. Dare he approach Captain Ashpen once more?

He took a breath, stepping forward from the rest of his squadron P-Ones.

"Captain Ashpen, sir," Daeson called.

Ashpen turned a fierce gaze Daeson's way.

"Forgive me, sir. I have information that will significantly impact our squadron's success. May I approach?"

Ashpen turned to Lt. Melzar. "Remind me—why did you recommend this one?"

Melzar tapped on his glass tablet and held it up for Captain Ashpen to see.

"His scores are the best I've ever seen, sir."

Ashpen turned his head toward Daeson. "Approach."

Daeson covered the few steps between them quickly, hoping to convince the man before drafting recommenced.

"Captain, two of those pilots are with me. I will personally vouch for their skills. I don't know what's in store, but if you need compatible pilots with an ability to coordinate aerial combat maneuvers, you'll want them. They won't let you down."

Ashpen stared at Daeson with steely cold eyes. Daeson wasn't sure if he was thinking about his proposal or if he was getting ready to be rid of him. He finally crossed his arms, squinted his eyes, and leaned forward. "If any of them fail me, you fail me. I don't care how good your scores are. Are we clear?"

"Very, sir."

"Lt. Melzar, submit a draft request for the two P-Ones he recommends."

Daeson stepped up beside Melzar. His tablet displayed headshots of each of the new P-Ones.

"That one and that one," Daeson said, pointing to Tig and Kyrah.

Melzar nodded. He quickly tapped and submitted a draft request for both. Daeson silently petitioned for Ell Yon to intervene on their behalf. A few minutes later, Tig and Kyrah were walking their way. Daeson could hardly contain himself, and he knew that Raviel was feeling the same. When they were within a few paces Tig and Kyrah recognized Daeson and Raviel. Their faces lit up, but their reunion was cut short by Ashpen's orders to stand at attention. Their story of survival would have to wait.

"Your training as Thunder Squadron pilots starts now. Prefect Zar, in his infinite wisdom, is on a quest to rule the galaxy, and he will succeed. Llyonian combat forces are the best in the galaxy, and you are going to help make them undefeatable. We will evaluate your skills in real-life combat exercises to determine which of you are worthy enough for us to learn from. Most of you will die. Out of twenty-five in my last squadron, two survived. Should you be eliminated from the P-One program because of your performance, you will be sent to work in the diconium mines for the rest of your short miserable lives, so I suggest you give us your best."

Captain Ashpen paused, scrutinizing the varied responses from his new recruits.

"Take a look at the rest of those squadron pilots out there," he ordered, waving his hand across the expanse to encompass the other seven squadrons. "At the end of your training, the trials will commence where you will fight against them. You will either kill or be killed. Should one or two of you survive, you will be granted the privilege of offering instruction to Llyonian pilot trainees and in some instances, experienced pilots, in order to hone our skills as the superior force in the galaxy."

Ashpen gazed at the stolid faces looking back at him.

"This is your new life. Consider it an honor to serve Prefect Zar in this noble way." He looked directly at Daeson. "Don't let me down or you will regret it!" He paused to let his words of warning linger. "Lieutenant Melzar will coordinate, track, and perform evaluations of your daily performance. All of my instructions will be passed through him. Any requests you may have to enhance your training will pass through him. Am I clear?"

There were a few "yes sir" responses from the stunned group of pilots.

"Am I clear?" Ashpen shouted, veins popping out from his strained neck.

"Yes sir!" came the unified voices of twenty-seven pilots.

When they arrived back at their quarters, the reunion for Daeson, Raviel, Tig, and Kyrah was joyous in spite of their dismal future.

"Thank Ell Yon you two survived!" Daeson exclaimed. "I saw your Starcraft go down and didn't see an ejection."

Tig took Kyrah's hand. "It was close...too close. Kyrah's leg was broken in two places."

"Their medtech abilities are incredible," Kyrah piped in, rubbing her thigh where one of the breaks must have been. "In just a few days my leg was nearly perfect."

"We were both pretty beat up," Tig added. "They worked on us for nearly a week, and I wasn't sure why. But then one of the medtechs said it was because we were pilots. Now I understand."

Raviel leaned out, putting a hand on Kyrah's knee. "I can't tell you how overjoyed we are that you're okay." Her hand dropped away, and her gaze fell to the floor. "I'm so sorry—we're all prisoners because of me."

Daeson wrapped an arm around her. "Hey, we're prisoners because of the fickle and wayward hearts of our people."

"He's right, Raviel," Tig said. "This isn't your fault, and we'll get through this. Ell Yon is with us, even here."

Later that afternoon, Lt. Melzar briefed the squadron on dozens of procedures and implemented a tightly structured schedule that began each morning at first light. On the first day, they were all issued dark blue P-One uniforms that were a cross between a utilitarian flight suit and a space suit with white stripes that ran from the wrists up the arms and to the neckline. They were also issued glass tablets that stored an endless litany of regulations and rules they were to memorize. This would also eventually store the operational manuals for the craft they would fly. On day two, their training and evaluation began. No longer was there any secrecy about what their roles would be—Captain Ashpen made that quite clear at every opportunity. They were first taken to a hangar that looked like it could be converted to a concert hall with minimal effort. Daeson and his team gawked in wonder at the sheer elegance. And if the hangar wasn't enough, the flying machine they were walking toward was a stunning piece of technology. Dark sleek lines silhouetted its form until the brightening lights of the hangar illumed its full stealthy shape. And they weren't the only ones mesmerized by its draw. All twenty-seven pilots of the Thunder Squadron encircled a single-seat, twin-engine craft of elegance and power. Lt. Melzar seemed to enjoy the expressions of the admiring pilots.

"Saw one of these on my six," Tig whispered. "Don't ever want to see that again."

Smaller than anything Daeson had ever flown, he could only imagine the extreme maneuverability of the craft. The thing most curious about it was the unique symmetry from the front of the craft to the back. At a distance, one wouldn't be able to tell if it was coming or going. The wings attached beneath the cockpit then reached forward and aft as if yearning to split the air in both directions. Two cannons of some unknown technology were positioned left and right of the cockpit just above the wings.

"We get to fly this?" one of the pilots asked.

Captain Ashpen reached for and stroked the slivered edge of one wing.

"This is the Shriek. The aerotech engineers that designed it were centuries ahead of their time. Small, fast, nimble, powerful...there is nothing like it outside of the Llyonian Fleet. Statistically, less than half of you will make it far enough in the evaluations to fly her, but I wanted to show you what you're shooting for. We start by training you on the Shriek's systems and capabilities. Those who master that will advance to simulation evaluations. Those who can endure the simulations will advance to the combat flight trials."

"Endure simulations?" asked one pilot.

Lt. Melzar looked his way. "We conduct simulation flight combat scenarios with the Shriek so as not to risk losing craft due to underqualified pilots. To ensure our simulations are accurate and realistic, pain due to projected bodily injury is also mimicked."

The inference stunned the pilots. Many began murmuring.

Captain Ashpen turned, glaring at the pilots. "We will have your best, and realistic simulations are just one way to ensure that. Dispense with any pilot arrogance you bring because you are prisoners of the Llyonian Empire, and you're in a fight for your very lives."

Ashpen's cold reminder subdued just about all giddy apprehension in regard to the Shriek, but there was an anticipation in Daeson that could not be tamed.

"Pay attention as Lt. Melzar details the capabilities of the Shriek," Captain Ashpen ordered.

Lt. Melzar stepped forward. "Aerodynamically the Shriek is an extremely capable and maneuverable craft in space and in atmosphere. Many of our experienced pilots describe it as a flying turret. The air foils are capable of flight both forward and backward. The cockpit, engines, and arc cannons pivot three hundred and sixty degrees to allow target acquisition and firing in any direction as well as near instantaneous flight vector changes. Advanced cockpit inertial dampeners allow for rapid deceleration and g-force endurance during corner maneuvering tactics."

"Are you saying this thing can fly forward *and* backward even when in atmospheric flight?" Tig asked.

"Technically speaking, yes," Melzar answered. "Our engine technology is independent of air flow so pivoting the cockpit and engines during flight allows an instant change in flight vector. But you'd better make sure your inertial dampeners are functioning or you'll end up splattered all over the cockpit."

Daeson grimaced. The visual was unpleasant.

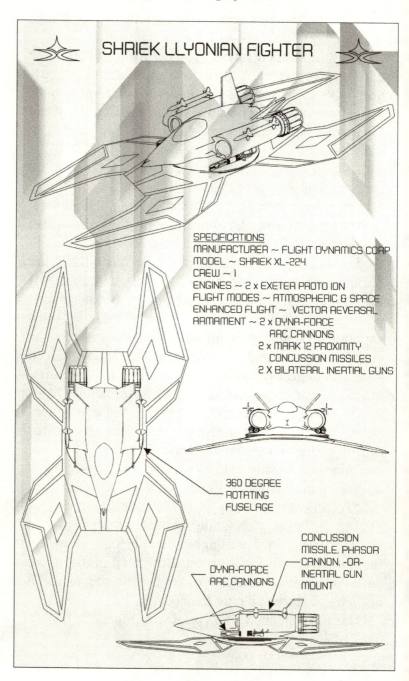

SHRIEK LLYONIAN FIGHTER

SPECIFICATIONS
MANUFACTURER ~ FLIGHT DYNAMICS CORP
MODEL ~ SHRIEK XL-224
CREW ~ 1
ENGINES ~ 2 x EXETER PROTO ION
FLIGHT MODES ~ ATMOSPHERIC & SPACE
ENHANCED FLIGHT ~ VECTOR REVERSAL
ARMAMENT ~ 2 x DYNA-FORCE
ARC CANNONS
2 x MARK 12 PROXIMITY
CONCUSSION MISSILES
2 X BILATERAL INERTIAL GUNS

360 DEGREE
ROTATING
FUSELAGE

CONCUSSION
MISSILE, PHASOR
CANNON, -OR-
INERTIAL GUN
MOUNT

DYNA-FORCE
ARC CANNONS

"And the cannons?" Kyrah piped up.

"The Shriek is equipped with dual dyna-force arc cannons. Two more hard points can be fitted with class 2 phasors, Mark 12 proximity concussion missiles, or the less preferred bilateral inertial guns."

Daeson couldn't help noticing the smile that spread across Kyrah's face.

Lt. Melzar continued to coach the pilots on the rest of the capabilities of the Shriek. It was a supremely impressive craft. When he was done, Captain Ashpen stepped forward again.

"Learning to fly the Shriek will test your piloting skills beyond anything you've experienced so far, but that's just a part of what we're looking for. Ultimately, we are searching for skilled pilots that are tacticians…strategists. That's where PCM takes over, Pilot Combat Maneuvering. Essentially, we will be evaluating your ability to apply all available resources to exact the best outcome in a battle. It means utilizing and relying on other skilled pilots and their weapons to win the day. That's what the PCM trials determine for us. This quest allows us to continue to expand our knowledge and maintain our dominance in the galaxy. It is Prefect Zar that makes us so!"

Daeson noted that the reverence for Zar superseded mere respect for a successful leader. It caused no small amount of uneasiness within him. He glanced toward his companions and noticed the same concern in their eyes. Only time would tell how such a culture of mortal admiration would clash with their pledge to honor only Sovereign Ell Yon in such a way.

CHAPTER

12

Simulations That Kill

Inertial Dampener – an anti-grav device designed to counteract the effects of inertia caused by movement and acceleration.

Inertial Amplifier – an anti-grav device designed to induce inertial forces typically on a body at rest.

B y the end of their first week of training, Daeson became acutely aware that Raviel's and Kyrah's survival was going to depend on how quickly and effectively he and Tig could enhance their piloting skills. Sitting in one of their Shriek maneuverability instructional classes, Daeson scanned the other pilots. He dared not view them as the enemy, or even as competition. He reminded himself that every one of them were prisoners just like they were. He resolved to help anyone that asked, no matter the outcome. After all, it was the Navi way.

As the day to begin simulation training approached, Kyrah looked concerned.

"I'm nowhere near your skill level as a pilot."

Tig consoled her. "We're all in this together, and we're going to get through it together."

"Tig's right," Daeson added. "You're a trained combat soldier with leadership experience and keen battlefield situational awareness. The mindset of strategy warfare is the same no matter the arena. We just have to get you through Shriek sim training, and you'll be okay. The truth is, we're all going to need each other to get through this."

Kyrah smirked.

"I'm serious," Daeson countered. "No one knows craft systems like Raviel, and you're a weapons expert, Kyrah. Tig and I know piloting and tactics. We are going to have to rely on and teach each other in order to survive. When we get to Pilot Combat Maneuvering, I will teach you everything the Malakians taught me."

This seemed to help Kyrah, and that is exactly what they did. The four of them didn't miss a single moment to encourage and train each other to maximize their potential as combat pilots. When other squadron pilots saw their cooperative efforts, many joined them to mutually support and enhance their survival in the program. When Lt. Melzar first saw what was happening, he approached Daeson, a look of bewilderment on his face.

"You're helping other pilots? Potentially at your own demise? Why would you do this? You're leading the squadron in every area."

Daeson saw a good heart in the man, in spite of his position as their captor.

"We follow the ways of Sovereign Ell Yon. To offer help to one in need is our way. I can't think of anyone more in need than a prisoner trying to survive the day."

Lt. Melzar looked incredulous. "I've never heard of such a thing. I'll need to report this to Captain Ashpen."

"Just remind Captain Ashpen that mutual support wins battles."

Melzar flashed a nervous smile.

"Lt. Melzar, Captain Ashpen said that we could make requests of you if those requests enhanced our training."

"Yes," Melzar said hesitantly.

"I and three of my fellow pilots are sworn to abstain from Deitum Prime. We haven't been taking the supplements given us each morning—"

"What?" Melzar exclaimed.

"Our performance is acceptable, is it not?" Daeson asked.

"Yes, but to refuse—"

"In addition to declining the supplements, I am requesting that we be given food and water that is free from Deitum Prime as well. I can personally guarantee that you'll have four pilots that will bring great honor to you and the captain as a result of our performance."

"There's no way Captain Ashpen would allow such a thing," Melzar protested.

"Test us then. Let us try this for ten days and see if you aren't convinced yourself," Daeson entreated.

Melzar rubbed the back of his neck, eyeing Daeson closely.

"I'll see what I can do. You'd better be right, or this could be the end of us both."

"This will work...you have my word."

When the ten-day trial was over, Lt. Melzar was forced to admit that Daeson was right. He, Tig, Raviel, and Kyrah were outperforming the rest of the squadron pilots in nearly every way, and so Melzar continued to honor Daeson's request for food free from Deitum Prime. As the days became weeks, the four won the favor of not only Lt. Melzar but also of Captain Ashpen. Their unassuming confidence, humility and demonstrative respect were distinctly unusual and refreshing in this cutthroat life-for-a-life culture.

When it was time to begin testing their skills in the full-up Shriek simulators, eleven of the squadron's original twenty-seven pilots had been eliminated. Captain Ashpen and Lt. Melzar took their remaining sixteen pilots to the Llyonian Flight Training Simulator Facility for their introductory rides.

"I never cared much for simulators," one of their fellow squadron pilots commented as they were getting ready to disembark the shuttle.

Daeson nodded. "They're just no match for the real thing."

"Who knows, maybe the Llyonians figured it out," Tig added.

"By the sounds of it, they've figured out how to match pain," Kyrah said with a smirk.

They were escorted into a massive building spanning over 300,000 square feet. Once again, every pilot was in awe at the magnificent design of the complex. The central section of the building housed the Grid, the galaxy's most advanced quantum computing technology along with an energy generation station large enough to power a small city. The powerful computing tech was required to perform the rigorous and elaborate simulation equations to replicate authentic atmospheric and space flight of the Shriek. The energy generation station powered not only the computational tech but also hundreds of gravitational amplifiers designed to emulate g-forces experienced by the pilots in every orientation of flight. From the Grid, three facility wings extended radially outward like spokes, each housing twenty-four Shriek simulators. Captain Ashpen led them from the Grid to one of the wings. They were greeted by a spectacle of tech wonder none had ever seen before. Lt. Melzar stepped forward to showcase one of the simulator stations.

"This is Shriek Simulator Arena Alpha. There are identical simulation arenas in each adjoining wing, arenas Bravo and Charlie." Melzar pointed to the center of the facility and then outward from the Grid. "When you compete against other squadrons, they will be flying in those arenas."

The P-Ones gathered around one simulator station that teased their eyes with curiosity. Lt. Melzar flipped a switch which energized the station. Ribbons of light outlined a bullet-shaped cockpit secured on a lower pedestal inside a spherical geo-structure with six arc antenna structures. The structures were equally spaced around the cockpit, attached at the base, and nearly touching just above the cockpit.

"Each Shriek simulator has a fully functioning cockpit," Melzar continued. "Just as an actual Shriek has inertial dampeners to reduce the effect of g-forces during maneuvers, the Shriek simulators conversely have inertial amplifiers to induce the effect of those same g-forces thereby emulating realistic flight. The arc-shaped structures are perfectly controlled inertial amplifier antennas positioned and controlled in a spherical orientation to perfectly replicate your maneuvers. There is no real-life motion this simulator can't replicate."

SHRIEK SIMULATOR

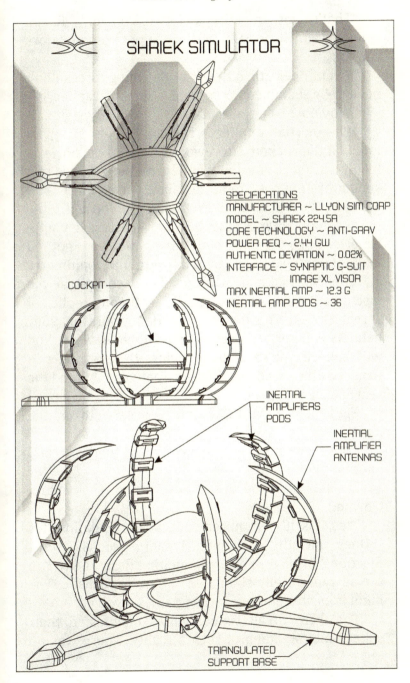

SPECIFICATIONS
MANUFACTURER ~ LLYON SIM CORP
MODEL ~ SHRIEK 224.5A
CORE TECHNOLOGY ~ ANTI-GRAV
POWER REQ ~ 2.44 GW
AUTHENTIC DEVIATION ~ 0.02%
INTERFACE ~ SYNAPTIC G-SUIT
IMAGE XL VISOR
MAX INERTIAL AMP ~ 12.3 G
INERTIAL AMP PODS ~ 36

COCKPIT

INERTIAL
AMPLIFIERS
PODS

INERTIAL
AMPLIFIER
ANTENNAS

TRIANGULATED
SUPPORT BASE

"That's got to take a lot of power," Raviel commented. "Especially with seventy-two simulators running."

"Yes, it does...thus the Grid. But the g-forces don't need to be sustained for very long." Melzar replied.

"Why not?" Daeson asked.

"The inertial amplifiers can create over 12 g's of force on the cockpit. However, because of the Shriek's highly advanced inertial dampeners, the g-forces in a simulator only need to be sustained for no more than 4.2 seconds, and at no more than 5 g's. Those are the inertial dampener's activation parameters. If you're experiencing more than that, you've got a malfunctioning dampener, and I certainly wouldn't try a vector-reversal maneuver. Inside the cockpit, all the instrumentation is an exact and functioning replica of a real Shriek. The image projection visors on your helmets will perfectly recreate the outside world. You will believe you're actually flying. Believe me...you won't be able to tell the difference between this and the real Shriek."

Tig leaned toward Daeson. "Impressive to say the least."

"You mentioned pain replication...is that for real?" another pilot asked.

Lt. Melzar looked to Captain Ashpen. The captain frowned.

"Yes, it is. It's a requirement that all simulations for P-Ones include authentic synaptic sensor suits. Ejections, broken bones, and melting flesh due to fire are all synaptically simulated and quite realistic. The mind is easily convinced when pain is involved."

The faces of all sixteen pilots manifested their sober understanding of such a reality. There was no room for apathetic training in the world of the Llyonians.

The first three simulation rides were basic non-combat flights to give the P-Ones the authentic feel of flying a craft that could respond unlike any other machine any of them had ever flown before. The simulator was indeed everything Lt. Melzar had said it would be. Visually, physically, and in every other sense, these simulators were perfect. It took Daeson a full three flights before he started to get the "pilot feel" for the Shriek like he had with the Starcraft. Tig followed suit, and Kyrah was quickly gaining ground too. For Raviel, the transition to flying the Shriek was nearly instantaneous.

"How is that you're able to adapt so quickly?" Daeson asked with envy.

"I'm not sure," Raviel replied. "Once I understood the mechanics of the design, it all just seemed to click."

"She also didn't have a thousand flight hours of previous habits to break that might inhibit her ability to adapt," Tig added.

"Very true," Daeson agreed. "Well, whatever the reason, I'm glad for it." He looked toward Kyrah. "It looks like you've got a good feel for it too."

"It's coming along. I'm looking forward to the next two flights...weapons deployment."

After five more flights, combat flights with the other squadrons began. The intensity of the training ramped up to overdrive. They began with 1v1 and 2v2 fighter engagements. Daeson quickly became thrilled with the capabilities of the Shriek. Pivoting, targeting, deploying weapons, vector reversal maneuvers...he felt nearly invincible in such a craft. During one engagement, Tig took a shot to his right wing causing his Shriek to spin uncontrollably. He ejected and survived, but the experience was memorable to say the least. Daeson landed, ran to Tig's simulator and helped him out. Tig's eyes were wide.

"Are you okay, Tig?" Daeson asked.

Tig swallowed hard. "I can't even begin to describe how realistic that was. I hate this suit. Can't imagine what a fire would feel like."

Daeson handed him a bottle of water. "Let's not find out."

Four weeks into the training, they began aerial combat maneuvering engagements and evaluations. Daeson led a four-ship flight from Thunder Squadron against a four-ship with Hammer Squadron. His number three was Raviel, each of them leading another Thunder pilot into battle. With Daeson's strategy, they quickly eliminated two Hammer Shrieks and were about to eliminate the remaining two. Seeing what he thought was an opportunity, Daeson's wing man broke formation and went in for the kill, not realizing that he had made himself vulnerable to the last Hammer pilot. One perfectly shot arc-cannon blew clear through the cockpit sending the pilot and his Shriek down in a ball of fire. Daeson, Raviel and her wingman quickly finished out the fight then landed. Daeson ran to his wingman's simulator, knowing the pilot would be dealing with lingering pain from his synaptic suit. The cockpit slowly opened to reveal that the man was unconscious. Daeson yelled for help. As he, Raviel, and their flight mate pulled the unconscious pilot from the cockpit, Captain Ashpen arrived. Daeson pulled the pilot's helmet off to discover that he wasn't just unconscious—he was dead. Daeson glared up at Ashpen, anger burning in his heart.

"How is this possible?"

Ashpen looked stern. "For some, simulated reality *is* reality, and the mind can destroy itself."

"Are you telling me that some of the pilots I've shot down over the last few weeks might have died...just like him?" Daeson slowly stood, facing off with Asphen.

Ashpen stepped forward, putting his face just inches from Daeson's. "This isn't a game...it never was. I told you this was a fight for your lives." He pushed a finger into Daeson's chest. "You are a prisoner of Prefect Zar's empire, and you will serve to bring him honor...in life and in death. Do I make myself clear?"

Daeson sneered. "Perfectly."

Back at their quarters, Daeson, Tig, Raviel, and Kyrah gathered to discuss the events of the day. Daeson shook his head. The reality of what his victories might have meant for his competitors was weighing heavily on him.

"We cannot be the instruments of death for Zar."

"We couldn't have known," Raviel said, putting a consoling hand on his shoulder.

"Besides," Kyrah added, "we only have two more simulations before we transition to real flights. How do you propose we fight and not kill then?"

All four of them had known this day was coming, and now that it was upon them, they were facing the worst of scenarios as Navi for Ell Yon. If they refused to fly, they would be killed.

"All I know is that I will not kill for an evil prefect making himself out to be higher than Sovereign Ell Yon," Daeson said, looking each of his companions in the eye. "Each of us have excelled in the training and are the top four pilots in the squadron. Let's be even better."

"What are you proposing?" Tig asked.

"Kyrah, help us figure out the perfect settings for our energy weapons that will disable the Shriek but not kill the pilot," Daeson offered.

Kyrah nodded. "I can do that, but a lot depends on where the shot hits."

Daeson looked at Raviel. She nodded.

"The Shriek is small, but our targeting system is so precise that with a little finesse, I think we can pinpoint certain sections of the Shriek, especially with a phasor cannon, but we would have to be no farther than one mile. The phasor cannons are less powerful but faster to target...nearly instantaneous. We'd have to be careful with the arc cannons—with a concussion missile, all bets are off."

"There is one more option for us," Kyrah offered. "What about the rapid-fire bilateral inertial guns?"

"Interesting thought," Daeson said. "The Llyonian aerotech instructors sure don't recommend them."

"Yes, but that's because they teach long-range weapon deployment. Our new strategy requires close-range engagements. It's a bit of an antiquated weapon that basically slings shaped cobalt projectiles at a target, but at close range and for what we're trying to accomplish, it just might be the answer. There are a few disadvantages, but the one advantage is that it has the ability to penetrate an E-shield much easier than an energy weapon."

"How many cobalt rounds can we carry?" Raviel asked.

"Five thousand each," Kyrah answered. "When they say rapid fire, they mean it. Even with 5,000 rounds you'll only have ten seconds of trigger time."

Daeson whistled. "Five hundred rounds a second!"

"I think it's a good call," Tig finished. "I recommend we arm with two arc cannons, one phasor, and one inertial gun fully loaded."

"Agreed," Daeson said. "We only have two sim rides left to perfect this. I'll draw up new tactics to pull our fights in close."

The last two sim ride evaluations were between each squadron's top pilots. Only nine pilots remained in Thunder Squadron. Daeson, Raviel, Tig, and Kyrah were their best, so they flew as a flight of four in each of the two remaining evaluation rides. After multiple engagements, they had accomplished exactly what they had set out to do...non-lethal victory in each of the last two engagements. After their last sim flight, the four gathered in a debriefing room where Captain Ashpen and Lt. Melzar joined them. Melzar eyed them with a new measure of respect, but Ashpen appeared indignant. He closed the door then glared at them.

"What do you think you're doing?"

"We're winning for you, Captain," Daeson replied, his face deadpan. Despite Daeson having won the captain's trust and respect, there evidently were limits.

Ashpen's eyes narrowed. "Don't be smart with me, Starlore. I know what you're up to, and you're going to disgrace me."

Daeson was surprised Ashpen even remembered his Raylean name. It was a sign that the man might be persuaded despite his frustration. Daeson used it.

"Captain, we're bound by a code that transcends anything here on Llyon or even our homeworld of Rayl. We will die before we break our honor with the Immortal Ell Yon. We will give you our best, but we will not intentionally kill innocent prisoners, even if they are trying to kill us, because they're not our enemy."

Ashpen's expression didn't change. "Who *is* your enemy?" He gazed at each of Daeson's companions in turn.

Daeson hesitated. "You wouldn't believe me if I told you, but it's not those squadron pilots out there, and it isn't even our captors. Look Captain, let us win the trials for you. Just let us do it our way."

Ashpen's face softened. He stared at each one in turn then looked at Melzar. "Get them our four best Shrieks, and set them up for their first flights." Ashpen glanced back at them. He looked like he was about to add some final remark but instead just turned and left the room.

Melzar smiled and shook his head. "I've never seen the captain at a loss for words. Impressive, Thunder pilots…very impressive. Just remember that tomorrow, all simulations are off. This is for real, so you'd better be sure about what you're doing."

Daeson knew that this type of flying was putting a significant extra measure of stress on Raviel, Tig, and Kyrah. Later that night, he found an opportunity to be alone with Raviel outside on the campus grounds.

"How are you doing, Rav?" he asked, taking her hand in his. "*Really.*"

"I'm doing well. But I have to say that I'm very thankful to have made it through the simulation rides without having had my synaptic suit go all zappy on me."

Daeson wrapped an arm around her. "Me too."

He and Raviel spent the next two hours enjoying each other's company under the soft glow of Llyon's two moons. It was a brief respite, for soon they would be facing the reality of live combat. Inwardly, Daeson was fearful for Raviel, wondering if at any moment she might slip into a spacetime event going Mach two. The mere thought of it caused him to tremble.

"Are you okay?" Raviel asked, wrapping her arms around his torso.

"Yeah…just a little chilled."

Raviel could hardly bear keeping her true feelings from Daeson. The truth was that she was in a constant battle to keep her fear under control. But there was absolutely nothing she or Daeson could do about it, and she also knew that Daeson was bearing the greater burden for the four of them…for all of Rayl, as their Navi in captivity. She didn't want to burden him further or distract him from doing exactly what he needed to do to get them on the other side of this. The reason she was so relieved regarding the pain of the synaptic suit wasn't because of the pain itself, but rather what that pain might do to her. She suspected that bodily stress or pain may be one of the time slip triggers that could initiate a slip into the future. That certainly wasn't always the case, for at least twice the event had come from nowhere, but whenever her pain reached a certain level, her grip on this reality seemed to loosen.

She felt Daeson shiver.

"Are you okay?" Raviel asked, wrapping her arms around his torso.

"Yeah…just a little chilled."

Raviel rested her head on his chest. *I'm not the only one hiding my feelings,* she thought.

CHAPTER

13

The Trials

Athough the Shriek simulators were expressly realistic, there was a thrill about strapping on a real fighter that no simulator could ever replicate. But before any P-One was given access to a Shriek, the remaining sixty-four pilots, eight from each squadron, were gathered into a large briefing room for a pre-trial briefing. Admiral Corsak, the director of the Llyonian Flight Training Facility, stood before them.

"P-Ones...you are about to begin our final evaluation of your skills as pilots and warfare tacticians. Should you survive these evaluations, you will be granted the high honor of becoming an advisor for the Llyonian Empire, serving Prefect Zar in the highest capacity. Be warned, should any of you be foolish enough to consider escape or to utilize your weapons in any fashion other than in accordance with the Trials criteria, you will be instantly terminated. Every Shriek has an auto self-destruct that will engage if you fly outside the boundaries of the Trial operating area or attempt to employ your weapons in an unacceptable manner. Each Shriek is navigationally tracked and monitored as well as each pilot via the implanted tracker in your shoulders."

Admiral Corsak paused. "Each of you will be allowed two orientation flights before the Pilot Combat Maneuvering Trials begin. During the Trials, every detail of your performance will be evaluated and showcased here."

The director nodded to an assistant who operated a control panel. The wall behind the director dissolved away to reveal a massive multi-level domed stadium that seated over 500,000 spectators. The briefing room they were sitting in was premier seating, front and center to some sophisticated display arena. The director lifted his hand toward the center of the stadium.

"That is a holographic projection field 1,500 feet long by 1,000 feet wide. It is a scaled representation of your actual trial's flight operating area."

Just then the projection field energized showing a perfect holographic representation of the terrain under their flight operating area. They could see a two-ship of Shrieks flying across the area. All at once the hologram zoomed in to show a near one-to-one scale of the flight. It was quite a spectacular visual despite the fact that, once again, lives would be lost for the sake of entertainment.

"Prefect Zar, our top military leaders, and 450,000 select privileged Llyonian citizens will attend the Trials, but the entire planet of Llyon and many of our subject planets will be watching via our holographic broadcast network. Whether you live or die during the Trials, you can take great pride in knowing you have served Prefect Zar the Great!"

There it was again. Daeson, Raviel, Tig, and Kyrah all exchanged looks of immense disdain for such misplaced adoration.

After the director's briefing, Daeson met with Captain Ashpen and convinced him to keep his flight of Raviel, Tig, and Kyrah together throughout the Trials in order to give their squadron the best chance at victory.

Their orientation flights all went well. Daeson had to admit that the simulators had indeed done their job since it was difficult to distinguish between their simulated flights and the real flights.

The next day, Daeson, Raviel, Tig, and Kyrah flew their first Pilot Combat Maneuver Trial against four pilots from Dagger Squadron. The eight combat Shrieks were positioned in the middle of the stadium prepped and ready for take-off. From opposite sides of the stadium, the eight pilots exited their briefing rooms and walked to their waiting Shrieks under the uproarious shouts and applause of half a million spectators. In perfect synchronicity, the ground crews signaled engine starts, then launched them one by one up and away from the stadium. Immediately after their departure, the center of the stadium transformed into a one-and-a-half million square foot holographic projection field.

Their first engagement was a strategic aerial game of combat chess that lasted twenty-three minutes, eventually digressing into separate 2v2 dogfight scenarios. Daeson and Raviel were successful in disabling both Dagger Squadron Shrieks, rendering them ineffective and unable to continue the fight. Tig and Kyrah did the same, causing one of the Dagger pilots to have to eject at the last moment before impacting the ragged edge of a mountain. The Llyonian evaluators and the stadium attendees were equally disappointed with the lack of dramatic "kills," but Daeson and his companions cared nothing for that. Captain Ashpen was furious, but Daeson was able to soothe his anger with a calm assurance of future victories.

After the next set of Trials, it became clear that Daeson and his three flight mates were purposefully sparing their competitors, often exposing themselves to great risk. The necessary skill and the finesse of their flying abilities to accomplish this was obvious to all at the Trials, thereby increasing the thrill and intensity of the combat flights to a level the Llyonians had never experienced before. By the third round, Captain Ashpen and Lt. Melzar were elated by the attention and accolades being afforded them as a result of the fantastic airmanship demonstrated by Daeson, Raviel, Tig, and Kyrah. Going into the final round of Trials, the stadium pulsated with the riotous rallying cries for the "Thunder Four." In their briefing room, Daeson, Raviel, Tig, and Kyrah could hear the muffled shouts of 500,000 spectators anxious to see them fly and fight once more. Captain Ashpen was actually smiling as he prepared his P-Ones for the championship trial. Lt. Melzar, too, was as giddy as a schoolboy. Apparently, Thunder Squadron hadn't made the Trial's championship in decades.

"Prefect Zar is pleased, and anxious to see you fight. You've done well, Thunder pilots," Captain Ashpen said. "Don't become complacent. I've seen these four Lightning P-Ones, and they're good...very good." His smile faded. "They won't hesitate to deal a kill shot to each of you."

Ashpen truly looked concerned, not just for the outcome of the championship Trial, but for each of them. "Fly smart, and be careful," he finished, his eyes softening.

Daeson, Raviel, Tig, and Kyrah all stood and saluted the man. Ashpen returned the salute then offered his hand to each, a gesture that stunned Lt. Melzar.

A moment later, the wall to their ground-floor briefing room dissolved, filling their ears with a near-painful eruption of cheers and applause. Daeson looked at his companions.

"You ready for this?" he asked. They each nodded confidently. "We have a unique plan that should allow us to avoid their long-range concussion missiles and get us close enough to wrap it up in a close fight, but plan on being surprised by them as well." Daeson couldn't help feeling apprehension. What his bonded and his friends had agreed to was birthed in hearts of nobility. "May Ell Yon grant us victory and life."

The four Thunder pilots stepped out from their briefing room and walked onto the stadium field in perfect military step. The roar of a half a million voices escalated until Daeson could nearly feel the sound pushing against his body. They marched to their Shrieks, each in turn firing up their engines waiting for the signal to launch. Moments later, the final eight Shrieks launched into the cloudless blue sky of Llyon. Ten minutes later, all eight Shrieks were positioned in the designated Flight Operating Area or FOA. Daeson and his Thunder pilot flight mates were positioned on the southern edge of the FOA with the four Lightning pilots positioned 250 miles away at the northern edge of the FOA. At 1400 hours, the "fights on" call was given—the Pilot Combat Maneuvering Championship Trial began.

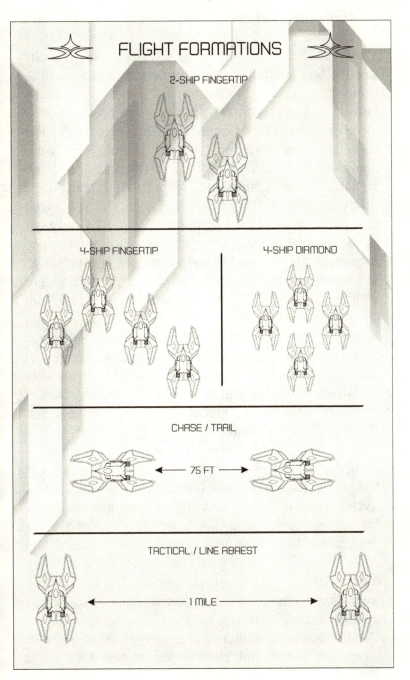

Line abreast at one mile spacing, all four Thunder pilots turned off their targeting and communication systems. Then they turned to a flight vector directly toward one another, flying at a perpendicular path to their approaching competitor Shrieks. This made getting a target contact and lock by the Lightning Shrieks difficult if not impossible. By turning off their targeting and communication systems, they were completely eliminating their electronic radiation signature so the Lightning Shrieks couldn't track them that way as well. Once Daeson, Raviel, Tig, and Kyrah merged to nearly a single point, Tig and Kyrah went pure vertical, flying straight up in a tight close formation. Daeson and Raviel went pure vertical down in a tight close formation as well. This had the effect of all four Thunder pilots merging and disappearing from the Lightning Shriek's targeting systems. Daeson and Raviel flew straight for the ground in a terrifying high-speed dive, pulling up at the last second with a painful 12 G recovery. The maneuver sent a wave of exclamation throughout the watchers at the stadium and across the entire planet of spectators. Now just thirty feet off the ground on a terrain-hugging, target-system-avoiding low-level, they flew east, straight for a bordering mountain range. High above them at the fringes of space and just below the FOA ceiling, Tig and Kyrah turned west, staying in a tight fingertip formation, giving the Lightning Shrieks the false impression that there was now only one target they could lock on to. Their goal was to close the distance quickly to keep the Lightning Shrieks from launching their deadly concussion missiles, and so far, it appeared to be working.

Daeson and Raviel were now hidden by the mountain range and closing the distance between them and the Lightning pilots fast. The problem was that they were just as blind as their competitors and had to guess at their locations, which was dangerous. Daeson and Raviel briefly pulled further east away from the mountain range, then arced back at a vector that took them perpendicular to the range so they could cross the peak ridge with minimum exposure. As soon as they crossed the mountain range, the fight would be on. Loosening their formation, they found the perfect place to make their crossing. Performing a 180-degree roll, Daeson crossed inverted with his canopy just a few feet from the jagged peaks while Raviel skimmed its peak upright. Once they broke over the mountain ridge, they reactivated their targeting and communication systems. Daeson's com channel immediately filled with the chatter of two fully engaged dogfights...Tig and Kyrah.

"Thunder Two, I've got a bandit at ten o'clock high," Daeson radioed on his channel with Raviel. "Attack him from above, I'll pinch from below."

"Copy Thunder One," Raviel replied. "Thunder Three and Four are engaged at vector 273, 32 miles. Any lock on the fourth bandit?"

"Negative, Thunder Two. Watch your six!"

Within seconds Daeson and Raviel were inside of one mile in a 2v1 engagement. The Lightning pilot was immediately defensive, but he was good. The sky lit up with arc cannon fire that passed just above Daeson's wing. The Lightning Shriek then executed a vector reversal, swinging his cockpit nearly 150 degrees about to get a lock on Raviel. Daeson executed his own vector reversal but only needed a 90-degree swing, so he quickly made the lock.

"Thunder Two, break right!" Daeson called.

He timed a double phasor shot perfectly with Raviel's break to the right. The phasor shots weakened the bandit's E-shield as Raviel locked on to his right wing and shot a short burst with her inertial gun. The cobalt projectiles penetrated the remaining E-shield with relative ease, tearing through the vessel's wing. The Shriek immediately lost control and began spinning wildly as it fell from the sky.

"Come on...eject!" Daeson said, waiting for an anti-grav shroud. Two seconds later the pilot ejected, beginning his gentle descent to the ground.

"Splash one bandit," Daeson called. "Let's get to Thunder Three and Four, but keep your head up...bandit four is nearby."

"Copy Thunder One," Raviel replied.

By the time they had closed to within a few miles of Tig and Kyrah's fight, they had both been successful.

"Splash second bandit," Kyrah radioed.

"Splash third bandit," Tig followed. "Anybody got a lock on bandit four?"

The four Thunder pilots merged in the central region of the FOA just as Raviel made the call.

"Bandit four circled back. I've got a lock at twelve o'clock high. Two concussion missiles in the air!"

They had been taught that the chance of evading a Mark 12 proximity concussion missile with a solid target lock was less than twenty percent. The missiles were 14 miles out and closing.

"Thunder One, there's only two missiles. Our best chance is to split four directions," Tig radioed.

Tig's logic was sound, but Daeson wasn't about to concede two losses...probably deaths. From somewhere deep inside him the smallest of whispers tickled his thoughts.

Ten Miles.

"Negative, Thunder Three. Rejoin to a tight diamond formation," Daeson radioed back.

The silence on the radio and the lack of repositioning in their current tactical spread formation was a clear message back to Daeson.

"Trust me, Thunder Flight...rejoin now!"

Raviel, Tig, and Kyrah all rejoined in a tight diamond formation with Raviel off his left wing, Tig off of his right wing, and Kyrah trailing just below Daeson.

Eight miles.

"Thunder One, in this tight formation those two missiles could take all four of us out." Raviel's voice sounded calm, but Daeson felt the tension from her.

Five miles.

"Target both missiles. When I call it, I want all four Shrieks to unload every remaining cobalt round from your inertial gun you've got. We're going to create a wall of metal for those things to hit. When you're empty, everyone break away. Acknowledge."

Three miles.

"Two."

"Three."

"Four," came their replies.

One mile.

"Fire!" Daeson ordered.

The sound of four rapid-fire bilateral inertial guns unleashing a wall of over 10,000 rounds of cobalt projectiles reverberated through the canopies of each cockpit. A fraction of a second later the four Shrieks split in a bomb burst of four directions. With the undersides of their Shrieks to the oncoming missiles, none of them could tell what happened. Daeson rolled 180 and pulled hard back on the stick to get sight of his flight mates. He saw a burst of smoke and fire in their space, and Daeson's heart sunk. Who had been hit?

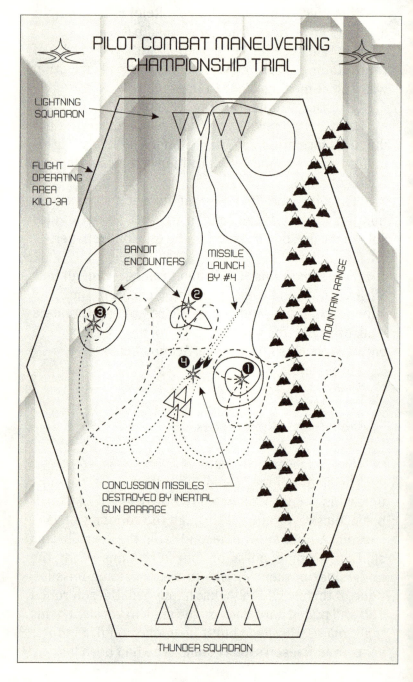

"Thunder Squadron, check!" he called.

"Thunder Three, check," Tig called.

"Thunder Four, check," Kyrah called.

Daeson waited, his heart pounding.

"Thunder Two, check, and I've got a lock on bandit four," Raviel radioed.

Daeson took a deep breath, grateful beyond words.

"Copy, Thunder Two, call it."

"He's straight and level…at cruising speed." Raviel's voice indicated surprise.

"Copy Thunder Two. I have the lock too. We'll go in with phasors hot. Thunder Three and Four, you fly cover and call hound dog if necessary."

"Copy", Tig replied, as Kyrah rejoined with him in a chase formation.

The four Thunder pilots closed the distance to bandit four in no time, but the last Lightning Squadron pilot wasn't making any evasive maneuvers. He continued to fly straight and level. Daeson dropped in behind him, targeting his right engine with his phasor.

"Thunder One, he doesn't even have his E-shield up," Raviel radioed.

"I'm going to check him out," Daeson replied. "Thunder Two, stay locked on back here."

"Copy…be careful, Thunder One, this could be a trick."

Daeson broke target lock, and accelerated up to fly beside the Lightning pilot. Now side by side the pilot looked over at Daeson, lifting his visor. Daeson did the same. The pilot then saluted Daeson, dropped his visor and accelerated, setting a course back to the stadium. Daeson and his flight followed him back where all five Shrieks landed amidst thunderous applause.

After Daeson, Raviel, Tig, and Kyrah exited their cockpits, the stadium crowd went wild with applause.

When the Lightning pilot exited, he approached Daeson and his flight mates, then bowed low in a gesture of respect. The crowd loved it, but evidently the Llyonian Flight Training Facility Director did not. Four Llyonian guardians quickly secured the pilot and whisked him away from the stadium. Shortly after that, Admiral Corsak, Captain Ashpen, Lt. Melzar, and a host of esteemed and powerful generals, admirals, and Trials officials came to personally congratulate Daeson, Raviel, Tig, and Kyrah. They were all escorted to a raised platform in the center of the stadium field.

"Congratulations to the new PCM Champions... Thunder Squadron!" Admiral Corsak announced triumphantly, his amplified voice echoing throughout the massive stadium. Captain Ashpen was allowed the honor of placing a Trials championship medallion around each of their necks. Afterward, directly in front of them, a section of the stadium looked as if it detached and began to float toward them. As it came closer, it became evident that this was Prefect Zar himself, ruler of the Llyonian Empire. The Director turned to face the four victorious pilots.

"When the imperial trumpets sound, you will bow down and acknowledge the Great Prefect Zar as the sole and all-powerful sovereign of the Aurora Galaxy and swear to serve him as your liege."

Daeson looked toward Raviel, Tig, and Kyrah. A look of solidarity filled their eyes as Prefect Zar's imperial platform continued toward them. When it stopped just 50 feet away, Zar stood and the crowd erupted in worshipful adoration. Then the sound of 200 trumpets filled the air with the Llyonian imperial flourish. All 500,000 stadium occupants and every member of the Trials entourage standing around Daeson, Raviel, Tig, and Kyrah bowed down onto their knees while lifting their right hands. With one eerie voice the stadium filled with a pledge to Zar.

"Hail, Prefect Zar, sole and all-powerful sovereign of the Aurora Galaxy. To you we pledge our allegiance."

All but four souls bowed and made the pledge...four Raylean prisoners.

When the pledge had ended, a terrifying silence filled the stadium as Zar and all of his subjects beheld the defiance of their newly decorated Trials champions. Admiral Corsak left his place and came to stand directly in front of Daeson, his face red with anger.

"You will bow down and acknowledge the Great Prefect Zar as the sole and all-powerful sovereign of the Aurora Galaxy and swear to serve him as your liege!" he said through clenched teeth.

Daeson looked past the director and directly up at Zar.

"We will not!"

CHAPTER

14

The Wrath
of Zar

The wrath of Prefect Zar was frightening. Daeson's words had kindled a raging fire of fury that the citizens of Llyon had never seen before. Captain Ashpen and Lt. Melzar stood stone cold off to their left with faces white with concern, fear, and worry. Surely they feared for their own lives as well, for these four profoundly skilled pilots were of their doing. Would they too endure the wrath of the most powerful man in the galaxy?

Five hundred thousand occupants looked on in fearful wonder as 20 Llyonian imperial guardians surrounded them. Prefect Zar glowered, peering down with a fierce countenance as he floated just 50 feet away on his regal throne of power, a sleek saucer-shaped platform equipped with anti-grav tech and an invisible energy shield. With him stood three admirals, two generals and three advisers, all attempting to mimic the fury of their prefect, but none could compare to the authentic blaze of anger in Zar's eyes. Unnatural silence hung in the air as Zar glared down on them. What would be the form of death for these insolent rebellious prisoners whom he had welcomed into his kingdom? Slowly he lifted his hand and pointed at them.

"Your insult to my empire is an insult to the whole of Llyon. I am the sovereign ruler of the galaxy! How dare you deny me the respect due me. All the world...nay all the galaxy will witness the consequence of such insolence! The method of your deaths shall be commensurate with the magnitude of your grievous offence."

Zar then lifted a fisted hand into the air at which time the massive domed ceiling of the arena began to split open in six directions revealing the brilliant rays of Llyon's two suns. As the arena opened its mouth to the sky, the unmistakable form of three star cruisers came into view as they descended from their lofty perches above. Daeson, Raviel, Tig, and Kyrah lifted their heads up to see the ominous sight. Daeson felt Raviel's hand slip into his. He looked into her eyes, feeling the angst within her, the very same angst he could not deny feeling in his own bosom. He stole a glance toward Tig and Kyrah. In some strange way, their exchange initiated an enveloping peace they could feel and see in each other—an acceptance of the end of lives well-lived for Sovereign Ell Yon. What better way to finish their life journeys than to display obedience and commitment to the one who had ordered their steps...to the one who was truly the author of power and of love throughout the galaxy.

The star cruisers positioned themselves in triangular locations, each one targeting two class 4 arc cannons at center stage of the arena—directly at the four souls who stood in defiance to the arrogant proclamations of the Prefect of Llyon. The 20 imperial guardians and the Trials committee members instinctively began to retreat away from the four prisoners as the voices of 500,000 onlookers exclaimed their astonishment. Surely Prefect Zar was bluffing. Six class 4 arc cannons to kill just four prisoners?

Zar lowered his gaze to Daeson and his comrades, allowing the intensity of the moment to build. He pointed his finger back at them.

"Kneel and proclaim me as your sovereign or be utterly destroyed!" he commanded, his voice echoing throughout the arena and broadcast out to the 28 planets under his control.

Daeson lifted his head upward then stepped forward.

"Zar, we will not be careful in how we answer you, for we serve only one ruler of this galaxy, and he is the Sovereign Ell Yon, who is able to deliver us from your hand if he so chooses. But if he chooses not to, let all of the galaxy hear and understand that we will not bow down to you though our lives be required of us."

Raviel, Tig, and Kyrah all stepped forward in solidarity to agree with the words Daeson had just spoken. At that time, Zar's rage possessed him so thoroughly that he screamed out profane words causing his accompanying admirals, generals, and advisors to retreat away from him.

"Destroy them!" he screamed, his face reddening to manifest a man crazed with near madness and imbued with copious amounts of Deitum Prime.

At this command, the entire arena gasped in horror as the sound of three star cruisers powering up their weapons permeated the air with a frightening crescendoing bass tone. The pilot of Zar's imperial platform quickly flew Zar and his entourage up and away from the ensuing micro apocalypse. The rest of the stage occupants and the 20 imperial guardians dispensed without any form of military decorum and began to run in all directions away from the center of the arena.

Daeson, Raviel, Tig, and Kyrah all joined hands.

"It has been the highest honor of my life to serve in battle and now in death with each of you. You are heroes for the sake of Ell Yon," Daeson declared.

At the pinnacle of the bone-shaking sound of impending doom, the air from above exploded in white-hot energy and consumed them thoroughly. Daeson closed his eyes in anticipation of his death as his world became instantly silent, but his thoughts did not cease. Showered in brilliant light, he felt the gentle squeeze of Raviel's hand in his. How could this be? He dared open his eyes to behold the most spectacular sight he had ever seen. Shrouded in the peaceful yet powerful blue sphere of Immortal protection, they were yet alive. He looked over at his companions, each one aglow with a supernatural effervescence that could only be authored by Ell Yon himself.

"What is happening?" Raviel gasped.

"Do not be afraid," came a powerful familiar voice from behind them. "I am with you!"

Daeson and his companions turned to see a most glorious sight...the valiant mighty form of none other than the Commander, his arms lifted up and hands outstretched, a Protector on each forearm bursting forth in unbreakable power against the forces of three star cruisers. It was the most magnificent sight that human eyes had ever seen. The Commander's face was set firm, his eyes ablaze with an eternal glow as he glared back at Zar. Daeson trembled at the sight of him and yet reveled in the demonstration of his power to the galaxy. This is the one they serve...this is the one whom deserved the honor and respect that Zar demanded, only the Commander didn't demand it. Such reverence was simply the natural response of beholding such perfection...such truth...such power.

"Commander," Daeson whispered in the silence of his protection.

The Commander's eyes softened as he accepted the admiring gazes of Daeson, Raviel, Tig, and Kyrah.

"Stay true. Stay strong. There's a future of peace and promise waiting for each of you."

All at once, the cacophony of colliding energy stopped, and the Commander disappeared in the blink of an eye. They each turned about to behold the chaos that such a reckless assault by Zar had caused. The scorched remains of the imperial guardians were scattered at various distances away from them. Other than for a 10-foot circular space around them, the entire center portion of the arena was scorched jet-black from the fierce power of the six arc cannons. Daeson looked up and saw one of the star cruisers veering off to its left, smoke and flames billowing out from one of the two arc cannons. People were screaming and running in all directions. Zar's imperial throne platform was swerving erratically as its pilot was desperately trying to land it safely. Suddenly, it careened into one of the lower sections of the grandstands, killing dozens beneath its fall. Zar no longer wore the face of contempt and anger. Instead, his face was white with fear. Daeson, Raviel, Tig, and Kyrah stood still amidst the ensuing chaos, beholding the spectacle of salvation and judgment at the hand of the Commander.

With the help of his advisors, Zar was able to disentangle himself from the platform's carnage. He pushed his helpers aside to make his way toward Daeson and his companions. He stumbled over debris and bodies to stand beneath what was left of the center stage where Daeson and his team stood. Zar looked up with eyes full of wonder and fear. The scene of the mighty Prefect Zar standing beneath the gaze of his four decorated prisoners caused all who remained in the arena to hush to silence.

"Surely the Immortal you serve is the true Sovereign of the galaxy. I saw his Commander standing with you, and there is none that could deliver you from such a death except that he be a ruler of all power." Zar turned about, astonished and afraid as if he were waiting for such a powerful being to appear and take his life. He shouted for all to hear. "Let everyone under my domain give honor and respect to the Immortal these four Rayleans serve, for he is the one and true Immortal Sovereign."

Zar turned back to Daeson and his companions, his face still full of astonishment.

"You will become rulers in my Llyonian Empire and serve with honor."

On that day, the fame of Daeson, Raviel, Tig and Kyrah went out to all worlds under Zar's rule, and the prefect was true to his word. They were each elevated to positions of authority and great responsibility, and through their influence, they were able to help many fellow Rayleans in their plight as captives. For a brief time, the enslaved people of Rayl discovered hope, knowing Ell Yon had not abandoned them completely, for there were Navi among them. As time passed, Prefect Zar came to trust and rely on Daeson, Raviel, Tig, and Kyrah greatly. They became instrumental in providing training for the Llyonian pilot program. The two primary training facilities for Llyonian pilots were located thousands of miles apart on two of Llyon's major continents. Daeson and Raviel were allowed to remain together, and part of their responsibility was to manage the facility at Benshik Beach Flight Center located on the northwest tip of the southern continent. Tig and Kyrah were responsible for the training at the Nebular Flight Center in the central region of the northern continent. Although still prisoners, they were initially given an unusual amount of freedom to implement their training techniques, including travel from one flight center to another. During one such occasion, Tig and Kyrah approached Daeson and Raviel with a request.

"How are you faring?" Daeson asked after the four of them greeted one another. They exited the hangar where Tig and Kyrah each had landed a Shriek.

"We're well," Tig said. "In spite of our apparent measure of freedom, I still can't convince our overseers to disengage the boundary auto-destruct on our Shrieks."

"I'm not sure that is *ever* going to happen," Daeson said with a side glance to his companions. "Perhaps they know where our hearts yet belong. Besides that, we still all have trackers embedded in us."

"I'm working on that," Raviel said in a hushed voice and a sly grin.

"We've sensed some extreme animosity among many of the Llyonian officials, but because of our favor with Zar, they're quiet about it for now."

"We feel it here too," Daeson said. "As long as Zar is prefect, we should be okay. In the meantime, there's opportunity for us to intercede and protect many of our people."

"Yes," Tig agreed. "But in spite of our privileged status, many of our people still suffer greatly. This can't go on forever."

"Ell Yon has put us in positions to help wherever possible," Raviel replied. "We must endure for as long as our people need us to." She then smiled. "Come, I have a lunch prepared for us."

Raviel led them to a pavilion on the flight center's western beach where the sounds of a vast ocean were a delightful backdrop, and the horizon stretched for as far as the eye could see. During the meal, they exchanged ideas, progress updates, and anything pertinent that might help them not only in their roles as flight training managers, but also in the way of assisting their fellow Rayleans. When the meal was over, Daeson noticed a subtle exchange between Tig and Kyrah.

Tig nodded and looked at Daeson and Raviel.

"Have you considered what might happen if Raviel has an episode here?" Tig asked.

Daeson reached for Raviel's hand. "Yes, we've given it a lot of consideration. I can only hope that Rivet has kept my Starcraft safe and out of the hands of the Llyonians. This situation certainly complicates things." Daeson hesitated. "The truth is we haven't been able to formulate a good plan, especially since we don't have access to a Protector."

"Without the Protectors, the people are beginning to feel abandoned. Other than the one Rimiah has, we don't even know where the Protectors are or if they've been destroyed." Raviel shook her head.

Tig and Kyrah nodded in agreement.

"It does seem as though each time you time slip that the duration you remain lasts longer than before," Tig noted. "I don't know if that helps or not."

"True, except for the very short time with Navi Lil and Prefect Luas, but I think that was an anomaly to the anomaly," Raviel said with a smile.

Daeson leaned forward. "Something else is on your mind...what is it?"

Tig and Kyrah both smiled. "Putting it mildly, the future is quite uncertain," Tig began. "And considering the challenges that we've just talked about, Kyrah and I want both of you to be part of something very important to us. We want to be bonded, and we'd like you to perform the ceremony, Daeson. As a Navi of Rayl, you are qualified."

"And we want for you to be our witness, Raviel," Kyrah added.

Raviel immediately jumped up from her seat and went to Kyrah. Daeson quickly followed.

"We're so happy for you!" Raviel exclaimed as the four of them exchanged embraces.

"Truly...we're honored to be part of your ceremony. When are you thinking?" Daeson asked.

"We were hoping we could do it right now," Kyrah said with a broad smile.

Daeson's eyes lifted. "Okay. Raviel, you'll have to help me, and hopefully I won't mess things up too badly," he said with a sheepish grin.

With a little preparation, the four of them were ready. On a foreign world, as prisoners of war, Tig and Kyrah were bonded. It was a brief respite from the ever-present sorrow of their captivity, for soon they would be thrust back into a world of woe.

CHAPTER

15

War in the Ruah

Tig's analysis of Raviel's time slip spans proved to be correct. Months passed with no indication that she was near to having a time slip event. Meanwhile, the people of Rayl continued to work as slaves for Zar and the Llyonians with no end in sight. One and a half years after Zar had promoted Daeson and his companions, the prefect took ill and died. There was a time of uncertainty as the military and political powers in place vied for control of the position of prefect. When it was over, a powerful and ruthless man named Azzar emerged as Prefect of Llyon, and the world of the Rayleans changed significantly. Forgotten was the edict by Zar to honor the Immortal whom Daeson, Raviel, Tig, and Kyrah served. Forgotten was Immortal intervention at the Capitol Trials Arena to save the lives of four Raylean P-One pilots. Daeson, Raviel, Tig, and Kyrah were removed from their positions as Azzar instituted new laws and positioned people he trusted into key offices, including the Flight Center management positions. Within just a few months, the burden of captivity fell heavily on the heads of every Raylean on the planet once more. Despair was preeminent as Daeson, Raviel, Tig, and Kyrah struggled to encourage their people. But before long, with all privileges removed, Daeson and Raviel completely lost contact with Tig and Kyrah. They found themselves as common workers at the Flight Center, completely removed from any flying duties. The Llyonian captivity began to wear long and hard on the Raylean people, for several years passed with no hope in sight.

"The plight of our people seems hopeless, Daeson." Raviel leaned into Daeson one evening as they considered the miserable state of their people. "Our people are desperate and persecuted. How long before they cease to even be identified as Rayleans? Are we being dissolved as a people?"

Daeson shook his head. "Without a Protector, I don't even know what to tell those who are with us."

Raviel's head hung low.

"I'm sorry, Rav. I feel the despair in our people too. But we must remember the promises of Ell Yon. Even if there are long periods of silence, his promises endure. Remember what he told us at the arena?"

Raviel looked up at him. "Yes...yes I do. How long though?"

Daeson pursed his lips. "I wish I knew."

That night, Daeson could not sleep. Deep into the midnight hour, his heart for the people broke. He lifted up his voice and his hands to Sovereign Ell Yon as though he were wearing the Protector and began to plead on behalf of the Rayleans.

"Mighty and Immortal Sovereign Ell Yon, we have all left your ways. You are merciful and keep your promises to them that honor and love you. All of the ways of the upright belong to you. We have been driven from our homeworld...the world you gave us. We are a desperate people, and we need you...we need your help. Please see us, mighty Sovereign, and deliver us for the glory of your name and your ways."

Daeson's plea continued long into the night until far away across the vastness of black space the hand of Ell Yon moved...

In the realm of the Ruah, deep at the edge of Malakian explored space, beyond Far Point, a fleet of majestic space vessels commanded by Admiral Galec was completing the resupply of a forward operating base.

"Admiral Galec," Captain Pallen, his first officer called. "There's an urgent secure priority one message from Tsiyyon."

"Patch it through to my quarters," Galec ordered as he exited to his bridge quarters and walked directly to the com center. Galec was more than curious regarding the communique. The war with the Torians had subsided for a time, and he knew that Admiral Kalem had returned to Tsiyyon to give the Commander a full situation report in person. Had something Kalem reported sparked this urgent message? Galec thought it unusual that Kalem's *Advent* Fleet had been stationed at Tsiyyon much longer than expected. Was this connected?

He fully expected to see Kalem on his display, but the First Admiral of the Aurora Galactic Fleet was not the one initiating the communication. When the image appeared, Galec snapped to attention.

"Commander, Admiral Galec reporting."

The Commander's eyes always surprised Galec, even when seeing them via a secure communication channel over a thousand light years away. There was a sense of infinite wisdom in them. It was frightening and reassuring all at the same time. The Commander paused. Galec then noticed Admiral Kalem standing behind and to the Commander's right. There must be some new assault by the Torians that needed reinforcements.

"Admiral Galec, I am contacting you because Dracus has effectively isolated the Llyonian controlled planets, and especially Llyon, from our forces. As you know, many of the Raylean people are in bondage there under a new prefect, Azzar. He brings harsh oppression on my people, and it's time. We've discovered Torian plans to use this evil leader to attempt to eradicate hundreds of thousands of the Sovereign's people. Daeson Starlore has petitioned Ell Yon for help. I'm sending you on a deep interdiction mission to deliver a message to the Navi."

Galec waited, never being quick to speak. He knew the deployment locations of the Torian Fleet. Penetrating Dracus's fleet forces in the Llyonian region of space would be nearly impossible. He would need more than his own fleet to accomplish the mission...and just to deliver a message? This was highly unusual. When the Commander appeared to have finished, Galec queried.

"Commander, the Torian forces there are significant. What will I have in the way of fleet force support?"

"Admiral Kalem will brief you on the planned tactics for the assault."

"If I may be so bold, Commander. Why not use the Protector to deliver the message? It appears we will be putting a lot on the line for just a message to a Navi." Galec inwardly winced. His words sounded less than respectful...and to the Commander! It was the primary reason he was usually slow to speak...too many times he had regretted an ill-prepared response. He opened his mouth to try to repair his blunder.

"Admiral Galec," the Commander said, intercepting his feeble attempt at a retraction. "The Protector was confiscated by Azzar, and the message that is to be delivered is to all Rayleans. There is no message given more important than what I am about to tell you. You will personally deliver this to Navi Starlore no matter the cost. Am I clear?"

Galec snapped to attention. "Yes, Commander. As you wish," he said bowing his head.

The Commander held his gaze on Galec a moment longer. He then touched the Protector on his forearm. "Message transmitted. Once you've memorized it, destroy all electronic evidence of its existence."

"Yes, Commander," Galec replied. He scanned the message text at the bottom of the display, quickly swiping it to transfer it to his personal glass tablet. Once he'd finished reading it, he slowly looked up, but the Commander was gone. Admiral Kalem stood in his place.

"I don't understand. How can this be?"

Kalem's eyes were unusually dark. "Do you now understand the significance of this mission?"

"I do, but I can hardly believe it. The risk to the Sovereign is...is..."

"I know, Galec," Kalem interrupted. "When C'fer first rebelled, I think Sovereign Ell Yon knew the depth of pain this was going to cause. Only now are we given a glimpse of what this truly means."

Galec considered Kalem's words. Despite their tenuous relationship many years ago, the great rebellion led by C'fer had forged a strong relationship built on trust in the two Malakians. Kalem had been chosen as First Admiral of the Aurora Galactic Fleet, and Galec had come to respect Kalem greatly.

"Humanity is this valuable to him?" Galec asked.

"You know the answer to that, my friend. And now we know what it looks like to truly love." Kalem paused, then stiffened. "We have much to plan and little time to do it. The Commander has chosen you and you alone to accomplish this. Are you ready?"

"With every fiber of my being, Admiral. What do you have?"

Within 24 hours, the forces for the deep interdiction strike were in motion. Galec initiated a communication blackout for his entire fleet from aboard the flagship, *Torrent*. He then turned in his captain's chair to the communications officer, Ensign Carmel.

"Open a fleetwide channel."

"Aye, sir. Channel open," the female officer replied seconds later.

"*Resolute* Fleet, this is Admiral Galec. We've been given a Code Alpha directive from headquarters on Tsiyyon. All communication outside the fleet is prohibited until our mission is complete. Ready all combat stations, arm all weapons hot, secure all docks, and prep all fighters. This is a deep interdiction strike into Torian controlled space. We launch in 20 minutes."

Every officer on the bridge turned to look at their Admiral...waiting.

"Lieutenant Margo, set a course for the planet Llyon in the Fraytis System via conduits Xray 12, Beta 6A, and Delta 4C. Transmit the planned route and coordinates to all other fleet vessels."

All eyes opened wide. They knew what this meant. There was no region of space more heavily occupied by Lord Dracus and his Torian forces than that of the Faytis system and its neighboring systems.

"Course laid in, Admiral," Margo replied.

"Ensign Carmel, notify me as soon as every vessel in the fleet has reported ready," he ordered, looking toward his com officer.

"Aye, Admiral," she replied.

"Captain Pallen—in my quarters," Galec ordered.

Behind closed doors, Galec briefed the captain on a few key facets of the mission, but only those necessary to accomplish his portion of the mission. The captain was a reliable man and accepted orders without question. But when Galec told Pallen to have one fighter aboard their flagship fueled, armed, and made ready, the captain hesitated.

"This isn't a request, captain...it's an order."

"Aye, sir. Any particular fighter?"

Galec eyed Pallen. "Yes. When we exit conduit Beta 6A, we will be receiving one fighter from the *Advent* Fleet. That's the one."

Pallen nodded, and the two men returned to the bridge.

Twenty minutes later, 25 vessels and a host of fighters of the *Resolute* Fleet entered their first slipstream conduit on their way to battle. What none of the 10,350 personnel knew was that their admiral would be placing himself at the leading edge of the battle...alone.

Intelligence reports indicated that the slipstream conduit near the Fraytis System's outer planetary body, a large gas giant, was the most accessible. Just before making the final jump, Admiral Galec addressed the fleet once more.

"Gallant crew of the *Resolute* Fleet, on the other side of this slipstream conduit gateway lies a fierce battle. Sovereign Ell Yon and the Commander have entrusted this most critical mission for humanity to us. In time, you will understand the significance of what we have been called to do here today. Our mission objective is to secure the region of space in proximity to the gateway. They will outnumber us, but we will have the element of surprise. I expect every crew member and every pilot to give their all." Galec paused to look at Captain Pallen. "All fighters launch, all hands...battle stations!"

A few minutes later, Ensign Carmel turned to face the Admiral. The look of apprehension in her eyes was unmistakable.

"All fighters have been launched and all vessels reporting ready, Admiral."

"Lt. Margo, take us in," Admiral Galec ordered.

Travel time through the conduit would be just under three minutes. As the space behind them melted away and the inner walls of the conduit dazzled its travelers with a brilliant display of iridescent streaks of light, those three minutes seemed to last forever. The entire bridge crew held their breath in anticipation of the scene that would materialize before them in just a few seconds. How many Torian battleships would be waiting?

"I want targets locked on the moment we're through. Is that clear, Lt. Brosenal?" Galec asked his sensors officer.

"Aye, sir. Sensors set to scan full spectrum."

All at once, the space in front of them resolved. For one brief moment the silence was surreal. Targets began filling the forward display identifying one battleship, one destroyer, three frigates, and four smaller assault vessels.

"Spread to attack formation. Target that battleship with all heavy cannons. Fighters take out those frigates," Galec commanded. "I want cover support from our port and starboard cannons for the rest of the fleet until every vessel is through the gateway."

The bridge erupted in a flurry of activity as the space before them filled with a barrage of plasma cannon and phasor bursts. The Torian forces immediately began returning fire, but the element of surprise was indeed proving to be an advantage for the Malakians...at least at first. Once all 25 vessels of the *Resolute* Fleet were through the gateway, the battle swayed heavily in Galec's favor.

"What do long-range sensors show?" Galec demanded.

Lt. Brosenal turned to look at his admiral, his face filled with concern.

"Two star cruisers, nine battleships, eight destroyers, 28 frigates and too many fighters and support vessels to count, Admiral," the sensors officer reported. "There are at least two full fleets in the system, and who knows how many other ships are in orbit around planets and moons that we can't see."

"Admiral, the destroyer and two Torian frigates have been destroyed. Their battleship is heavily damaged. The rest of the vessels are in retreat. Should we pursue?"

"Negative." Galec turned to his nav officer. "Make course 224 mark 74."

"Admiral, those coordinates will take us to the planet Ria. I thought our goal was Llyon," Captain Pallen stated.

"Llyon is too protected. We'll draw them out," Galec replied as he concentrated on the force deployment locations on one of the forward displays.

"Aah...a diversion," Pallen said with a subtle grin.

Galec didn't break concentration as he studied the display.

"Admiral, a star cruiser and multiple battleships and destroyers are on an intercept course," Lt. Margo reported.

"Captain, keep the fleet in tactical combat formation as we reposition."

"Aye, sir." Pallen began coordinating with each of the fleet vessels to ensure they were in the best defensible formation.

Like the pieces of a chess board, the powerful vessels of the Malakians and the Torians moved to strategic locations, each side positioning themselves for the next strike. With the element of surprise now gone, power and strategy would determine the victor of the day.

"They're also positioning multiple battleships and destroyers at each of the four gateways in the system," Lt. Brosenal stated. "Any hope of reinforcements has just been eliminated."

"There's no way out either," Pallen added quietly so that only Galec heard. But it didn't matter—every officer on the bridge would have been thinking the exact same thing. Galec didn't respond. "Admiral…is this a suicide mission?" Pallen whispered.

Galec turned a steely-eyed gaze toward his first officer. "Stay focused, Captain. We have a mission to accomplish."

Pallen stiffened and nodded.

Over the course of the next 45 minutes, Torian ships fully secured each of the gateways and were sending an entire armada on an intercept course that included one star cruiser, five battleships, four destroyers, 18 frigates, multiple smaller support gunships and over 70 fighters. It looked to be a massacre. As the scene of Torian dominance unfolded, the atmosphere on the bridge became thick with angst. The Torians were within minutes of being in weapons range. The whole situation looked like an intentional slaughter. Captain Pallen grew frustrated and angry.

"Admiral, we're too far from Llyon to complete the mission, and we don't have a chance of winning this battle."

"We don't need to win, Captain, we just need to buy some time," Galec replied. "Signal all vessels to divert all power, including weapons, to their forward E-shields. Ensign Carmel, be ready to open a secure hyperlight communication channel, authentication one six Sierra four Alpha."

"Authentication confirmed," Carmel replied. "Channel ready."

The Torian armada was nearly on them. It was an overwhelming sight to behold. They were outgunned two to one. For every crew member in Galec's fleet, certain destruction was in front of them. How could they possibly survive the day?

"Admiral, we're being hailed," Ensign Carmel said.

Galec looked her way, eyes narrow. "By whom?"

"It's the star cruiser *Indominable* in orbit around Llyon," Ensign Carmel stated. "It's Lord Dracus."

Galec immediately felt anger well up inside him. He knew that encountering his ancient friend turned archenemy was a possibility, but in the throes of preparation for battle he had pushed it far from his mind.

"Put him on the forward display," Galec ordered.

The display immediately filled with the form of Galec's former friend, C'fer, now known as Lord Dracus, commander of the Torian Empire...deceiver, betrayer, destroyer, anarchist. Galec straightened in his chair.

Dracus slowly shook his head. "I can't for the life of me understand what foolish trick you're up to my old friend. Surely you know that you will all die today."

Galec kept an eye on the closing distance of the Torian armada. They were now seconds away. He just stared back at Dracus. The leader of the Torians leaned forward in his chair, a look of curiosity on his face.

"You're in a hopeless situation." Dracus's eyes narrowed, then a sly smile crossed his lips. "Is it possible that...you've come to join us?" The man's evil smile broadened as he considered it.

Several of Galec's officers turned and looked at their admiral with a look of shock. Was this a possibility? Considering the hopeless circumstance that he had purposely put them in, it seemed the only reasonable explanation.

"The Torian Fleet is in weapons range," Lt. Brosenal reported.

Galec lifted his chin, peering directly into the eyes of darkness.

"With my last breath I will fight you and declare your foolish and evil ways to the galaxy, Dracus."

The delight on Dracus's face faded away. "And your last breath will be today you insignificant—"

"Cut channel," Galec ordered.

The display immediately erupted in a nightmare of weapons fire all directed at them. The *Torrent* began to tremble from the barrage of weapons. Their shields were holding, but nothing could withstand such an onslaught for long.

"Should we return fire?" Captain Pallen asked.

"Negative, keep all power diverted to our shields," Galec snapped. "Ensign Carmel, open the hyperlight channel now!"

"Channel open, Admiral."

"Flagship *Advent*, this is Admiral Galec of the star cruiser *Torrent*. Do you copy?"

The following five seconds were an eerie mix of apprehensive silence punctuated by the battle sounds of Torian cannon fire.

"*Torrent*, this is Admiral Kalem. Relay exit coordinates now."

Captain Pallen and nearly every officer on the bridge watched dumbfounded. What could this possibly mean?

"*Advent*, make your exit coordinates 219.33 by 641.85. Be advised we are under attack."

"Shields at 72 percent," Lt. Brosenal reported.

"Standby," Galec ordered.

Ten long seconds passed, and then the galaxy changed forever. Thirty-six ships of the *Advent* Fleet materialized out of nowhere in a position behind and just within weapons range of the attacking Torian armada, their cannons and phasors blazing forth in an array of glorious rescue.

"Divert power back to weapons and open fire!" Galec ordered.

Now with two Malakian fleets firing all weapons in a gauntlet of destruction on the unsuspecting Torian vessels, pandemonium struck the enemy.

"How is this possible?" Captain Pallen asked incredulously.

"No time to explain now," Galec said, standing up from the captain's chair. "We have a battle to fight and a mission to complete. The helm is yours, Captain."

"Admiral...surely not alone."

"It's the only way," Galec said, with a nod. "If I'm not back in two hours, get my fleet back through the Delta 4C conduit. Admiral Kalem will stay with you until our fleet is through."

Pallen swallowed hard, then saluted. "Aye, Admiral."

Galec made haste to the launching bay of the *Torrent*. The one remaining fighter in the bay didn't look much different than those of his own fleet, except for a singular unusually shaped pod he didn't recognize located just aft of the cockpit. The flight crew helped him quickly strap in, and the pilot that had flown the fighter to them earlier at a previous gateway gave him a quick rundown of the new controls. Galec powered up his engines and launched from the bay. He circled back under the *Torrent* and away from the fray of battle, then set his course directly for the planet Llyon.

Admiral Kalem's arrival and subsequent delay at Tsyyion had been for the express purpose of outfitting his entire fleet with new hyperspace jump drives that the Malakian technology masters had been secretly working on for years. They had discovered how to encapsulate each ship in a quantum spacetime shroud much like a conduit using a newly developed hyperdrive engine. However, this shroud was able to travel with the vessel unlike a stationary gateway. It was technologically brilliant! Now Galec would discover for himself just how effective such technology would prove to be.

After entering the coordinates, he engaged the new hyperspace drive. He arrived at a suborbital position in Llyon's atmosphere almost instantly, struggling to quell the thrill of such a journey. This would indeed change everything. With full cloak engaged, he made his way to the capitol city where a single human by the name of Daeson Starlore was kneeling with upstretched arms, pleading for his people. Carefully, Galec was able to make his way to Starlore undetected. Standing before the man, Galec hesitated. There was a beauty in such complete adoration. Though human, this was a fellow being who understood the power of Ell Yon. Galec lifted his arms, joining briefly in the complete adoration of his worthy Commander. He then touched the interphasal module on his belt. Starlore's eyes opened, wonder filling his face as he beheld the mighty form of a Malakian Admiral. The man bent low.

"Do not bow to me, for I am just as you!" Galec berated. "Stand up, Daeson Starlore, for you are highly favored in the Ruah."

Starlore slowly lifted his head, eyes glowing with the knowledge of Ell Yon. He stood before Galec, silent.

"I am Galec, Admiral of Sovereign Ell Yon's Aurora Galactic Fleet. From the time you began to petition Sovereign Ell Yon on behalf of your people, I was sent to deliver a message. The lord of the Torians came to fight against me, but Admiral Kalem came to help that I might fulfill my mission on your behalf. Here is the word of promise from Sovereign Ell Yon...an oath to his people of Rayl..."

CHAPTER

15

Oath of Ell Yon

THE OATH... "I have not forgotten my people. The time of Deitum Prime and those who promote it will come to an end, and I will purchase my people from the curse of its mortality. The Commander will break forth onto the noonday of Rayl and restore that which once was. The nation of my people and the city of Jalem will be rebuilt, even in desperate times. From the decree to rebuild the city until the appearance of the Commander will be 483 years. He will appear for a time and be put to death, but he will endure forever. After this, the deceiver will cause many to be destroyed and will rule until the judgement of Ell Yon shall fall upon him." – Galec, Malakian Admiral of Ell Yon as given to the Navi of the Llyonian Captivity

T he words of the mighty Malakian warrior lingered in Daeson's mind. In a moment, the warrior had appeared, and in another moment, he was gone. Daeson contemplated the profound oath of the Immortal who loved Rayl, not fully understanding everything that had been said. He carefully transcribed each word that Admiral Galec had spoken, replaying the message over and over in his mind. Later he shared what had happened with Raviel. Although the oath of the Sovereign seemed far into the future, knowing that Ell Yon had heard and was present with them in these difficult times was all the hope she needed. They began to spread the words of the oath to all Rayleans that would hear them, and it brought comfort to many. A network of communication between Rayleans across the planet was eventually established, and they were even able to reconnect with Tig and Kyrah and encourage each other from time to time. Any efforts to unify and encourage their people were important since news of the state of their homeworld, occasionally brought by an off-world trader, was difficult to hear. Much of their planet and many cities, especially Jalem, were in ruin.

One night, seven years after they had been deported to the world of the Llyonians, Daeson was taken.

"What do you want?" he protested as three Llyonian imperial guardians demanded he come with them.

Though their weapons were not drawn, they made it clear that this was not simply a request. Despite their demand, the guardians looked unusually nervous. Raviel looked as if she was going to make a move, but Daeson shook his head.

"Are you the Raylean that speaks with the Immortal?" the lead guardian asked.

Daeson and Raviel exchanged quizzical looks. What a strange question for a Llyonian to ask.

"I am Daeson Starlore, a Navi for the Raylean people."

The guardian nodded. "Please, come with us quickly."

Raviel looked like Daeson felt...stunned.

"I'll come," he said, then turned and grabbed Raviel's hand. "I'll be all right."

After a 15-minute flight in an imperial shuttle, Daeson and his three escorts arrived at Prefect Azzar's palace. There were no security checks and no scans for weapons. Daeson was whisked straight to the banquet hall where Azzar was hosting a revelrous feast, or at least had been by the look of strong drink, lewd people, and foggy remnants of vaporized Deitum Prime. Hundreds of Azzar's guests were backed up against the walls of the hall, shock and fear on their faces. A dozen of the prefect's counselors and scitechs stood off to one side, each also wearing countenances of great apprehension.

Daeson scanned the room trying to assimilate what was happening. His eyes quickly lit upon the cause of it all. In the middle of the elaborate hall, Prefect Azzar was immersed in a cocoon of vibrant blue energy. A look of abject horror was etched across his face—his eyes wild with fear as if he'd been subject to some holy terror. He appeared frozen in a state of near paralysis. Four Immortal symbols glowing in a supernatural light swirled around Azzar on the outer edges of the blue energy sphere.

Daeson approached, the stench of lingering Deitum Prime filling his nostrils. Righteous anger filled his soul. Then Daeson understood in a moment what was happening. Azzar's left hand was clutching his right forearm, where the Protector was fully and immovably attached. The ache in Daeson's heart was strong...to see it here after such a long time!

"Is th...th...this the man?" Azzar asked, his body twisted in a state of frozen panic.

"This is the Navi of the Rayleans," the lead guardian said, stepping aside for Daeson to approach.

"There were le...legends of great power," Azzar winced as if in pain, his eyes briefly flashing to the Protector. "What does th...this mean? These other imbeciles are w...worthless. Tell me and release me, and I'll make you rich and powerful in my empire."

Daeson slowly walked around the spectacle of Immortal intervention. What a fool Azzar was. He could imagine what the judgement of Ell Yon would be on and in the mind of such a licentious man. Daeson stopped and beheld the glowing symbols floating around the captive man. He had seen these symbols once before, when Ell Yon had taken him through the dimensional shift gate to the Ruah.

"Keep your gifts and give your power to another. I will both release you and tell you the meaning of these symbols."

Daeson then carefully but deliberately reached through the blue sphere of Immortal power and took hold of the Protector. All in the room gasped, sinking further into the walls. He could feel the restrained power of the Protector pulsing its conviction into the synapses of Azzar. Daeson lifted, and the Protector yielded. The cocoon of energy collapsed and Azzar instantly fell to the floor, devoid of any strength. However, the four glowing symbols remained, created and suspended by some energy force inexplicable to even the most advanced humans in the galaxy. Daeson placed the Protector over his right arm, closed his eyes, and pushed downward. The warmth of Ell Yon's presence filled his soul. Everyone in the banquet hall watched in hushed silence as Daeson's face filled with

Immortal knowledge. He opened his eyes and looked down at the heap of bones and flesh at his feet.

"The symbols are Laq, Kor, Exo, and Sep. The Immortal Sovereign Ell Yon, the one true prefect of all that exists, has judged you, Azzar, and found you lacking. This very night your empire will fall, and you will be killed, for you have mocked Ell Yon. Two worlds will come against you to divide Llyon."

Azzar then lifted himself up, still clearly undone by his exposure to Ell Yon. He stared at Daeson, the Protector pulsating on his arm.

"You will be a ruler in my land, and I will give you the wealth you refused, for I am Prefect of Llyon!"

Just then, the ground trembled beneath their feet and sirens began to sound across the great capitol city of the Llyonians.

"Open the terrace wall!" Azzar exclaimed, stumbling toward the west wall of the hall. A few seconds later, a large portion of one of the walls retracted left and right revealing a massive balcony. The people in the hall emptied onto it to behold the beginning of their end. A thousand brilliant flashes of plasma energy lit up the night sky in a beautiful but ominous display of an invading fleet of spaceships.

Without anyone caring to restrict him, Daeson left the palace and made his way back to Raviel.

"What's happening?" she asked, greeting him at the doorway of their humble dwelling. She then looked into his face and saw it. Touching his arm, her eyes filled with the light of hope.

"Yes, he is here, Rav. And this," Daeson waved to the sound of a collapsing empire above them. "This is their end and our beginning."

By night's end, Llyon had fallen, conquered by the forces of the rising Syan power of a nearby system.

Within just a few weeks of the Syan conquest of Llyon, all former captives were granted the freedom to return to their homeworlds. There was great rejoicing among the Raylean people as the effort to return home began.

Daeson and Raviel rejoined with Tig and Kyrah in their own joyful reunion. Because of the respect they had earned among the people, they became instrumental in arranging the return of their people to Rayl. The resources and spacecraft on Rayl were extremely limited so Daeson, Raviel, Tig, and Kyrah used every ounce of influence to make arrangements for transportation for their people. They would first travel back and begin ferrying in whatever vessels were available.

"Do you think that Rivet is okay?" Raviel asked Daeson as they prepared to land their first transport on home territory. "It's been such a long time."

"If any droid could evade and survive, it's Rivet."

Raviel smiled as she looked out the cockpit window of their small transport. "I guess you're right—look who's here to greet us!"

When they disembarked, Raviel actually hugged the bot, and Daeson could hardly keep himself from doing the same.

"It is good to see you, my lady and my liege," the android said with a tone of human enthusiasm.

"And you my friend," Daeson replied. "It's *really* good to see you. Tell me, how's Viper One? Were you able to keep her?"

Rivet looked toward Raviel, knowing that Daeson's concern wasn't for the Starcraft, but for what it meant in the way of finding Raviel if she were to experience another time slip event.

"The Starcraft is intact and safely hangared," Rivet replied. "Navi Rimiah was very helpful in this regard."

Daeson took a deep breath. "Well done, Rivet."

It took many months to arrange the transportation of hundreds of thousands of Rayleans back to Rayl, and there were many that chose not to leave since they had assimilated into the Llyonian way of life. Some had even chosen to migrate to other worlds, but essentially the nation of Rayl was whole once more. Jalem was indeed in a state of ruin, just as the traders had reported, but there was a renewed sense of hope. However, having been decimated for years, the Rayleans had virtually no defenses to speak of. This set them up to be a target for bandits and marauders from all across this region of space.

The work of restoration was painfully slow and frustrating. For every two steps forward they made, a raid would occur that would set them back one. And then, as if by the hand of Ell Yon, through a highly unusual set of circumstances, word came from Syan that the ruling prefect of that world was sending resources and help to rebuild Jalem and the other major cities of Rayl.

As often seemed to be the case, the words of Admiral Galec were nearly forgotten by most, but for Daeson and Raviel, the decree of the prefect meant supremely more than that of rebuilding a city.

CHAPTER

17

Revelation

Hearing her father speak the stories of Sovereign Ell Yon once more rekindled a portion of that old passion she'd once had as a girl. But it felt different this time. Elias looked at Brae.

"You're tired," he said as she tried to hide a yawn.

"Yes, I think I need to sleep. Is that the end you wanted to tell me?" Brae asked.

"Not quite," Elias said. "I think the story's end would be best heard when you're well rested. Will you let me finish it tomorrow? I think it may help you."

Brae tried to smile, but something inside her felt broken. And because of it, she felt like a part of her relationship with her father had been broken too.

"Sure."

Elias stood and walked to the door.

"Good night, Dad," Brae called after him. "I love you."

Elias turned. He offered a weak smile. "I love you too."

The next morning, Brae woke up late. By the time she made it down to the kitchen, Elias was gone.

"Master Elias went to town for supplies," said one of the bots in a cold flat voice.

"Hmm," Brae responded, searching for a cup to fill with hot tea to start the day. She glanced the bot's way. Elias hadn't ever upgraded his old work bots, at least not as long as Brae could remember. There were now some pretty sophisticated androids that had been built, and yet Elias would have nothing to do with them. Perhaps it was his deep-seeded phobia regarding the AI wars he believed had happened. And so, she had been stuck with Squeaky, Clunk, and Wheeze, names she had given their three bots when she was a teen. This one was Clunk. He was standing motionless in the entry way of the kitchen, like an abandoned appliance.

"What duties has he given to you, Squeaky, and Wheeze," she asked, realizing that enough time had passed since she had arrived home, and it was time to get to work. Besides, work on the homestead would take her mind off of the difficult conversation she and her father had had last night. Were more conversations like that to come? Inevitably. Elias was an internal processor. Although he didn't respond much to the shocking words she'd spoken, she knew he would have a lengthy reply when he was ready.

Clunk began reciting a lengthy list of menial tasks that didn't appeal to Brae at all.

"Stop!" she commanded. "What tasks does Elias have that he needs to do?" she asked, knowing it was a long shot getting Clunk to provide any meaningful reply. The bot seemed locked up for a moment as its obsolete processor tried to find a response.

"Master Elias has been working on fixing a malfunctioning engine on the S-23. He is also—"

"That's it," Brae interrupted. "I'd love to get my hands dirty on something worthwhile. It's been too long. Clunk, disregard your previously assigned duties. You will help me repair the S-23 today."

Clunk seemed lost as he processed her command. "New duties recorded," the clunky old bot replied.

Brae shook her head. The bot probably wouldn't be any help at all other than to fetch tools for her, but at least that would save her time and steps.

Brae ate her breakfast on the porch and didn't bother to clean up since she would be covered in grease and fuel in short order. Before long she was beneath the S-23 on a mechtech gravity creeper with her arms deep into the belly of the craft. Even though she was on a fast track to becoming a master astrotech, she had a knack for this sort of work. She loved machines, especially those that could fly. Elias had always bragged on her when she was growing up. By the time she was sixteen, she was performing most of the challenging mechtech work around the homestead. Occasionally Elias would have to call in a real mechtech for something that was beyond her skill set, but she was always right at his elbow, watching and learning when it happened.

"The ion infuser coil is shot. Looks like I've gotta pull the whole engine to fix this one," she said out loud to no one. For some reason she found it helpful to talk her way through a challenging repair like this, even if there wasn't anyone other than an old bot around to hear her.

With Clunk's help it took her 45 minutes to break loose all the engine tie-points and connect the anti-grav hoist to lift the engine out of the S-23. By now her hands were nearly black and her face had grease smudges in a half a dozen places. The engine was now in a position to begin effecting repairs. Just as she was about to climb beneath the engine, Clunk began pulling the safety cable to her. Brae eyed the bot, curious about its actions.

"Master Elias always secures the safety cable when using the anti-grav hoist," the bot said coldly, its hand extended with the cable and securing hook.

Brae eyed the anti-grav hoist. He wasn't wrong. It was a procedure that her dad had always insisted on. It was a bit of an annoyance, but she obliged...usually.

She huffed. "Fine."

Brae grabbed the cable and hook, then found a place to attach it on the engine which was now floating perfectly still in a workable position. Brae crawled back on the mechtech creeper and slid under the hulking mass of metal, conduit, and electronics. She worked for a few minutes to detach the ion infuser coil, but it was jammed.

"Clunk, hand a pry bar to me," she called out, wiping a few drops of sweat and lubrication fluid from her forehead.

The bot was far too slow for Brae's liking, but he finally complied. Clunk stayed nearby, waiting for her next request. Brae positioned the pry bar in a place to give her the greatest leverage, hoping it would free the coil. She tried three times without success. She positioned her right leg against the engine housing, then gave it one more shot, but it still didn't budge.

"Hand me an extension lever," she called out to Clunk. The bot walked to the bench where the extension lever was but just then, the anti-grav hoist lurched. Before Brae could move, disaster struck. The hoist completely failed, tearing loose from one end of the engine. Brae tried to roll out from under it, but there was no escape. The 2,000-pound mass would crush and kill her. Just a fraction of an inch above her head, it stopped, but part of the engine had pinned her outstretched leg, and she couldn't move. The safety cable had helped, but Brae heard the steel fibers creaking and starting to snap. Brae screamed as the pressure on her leg turned to pain. She turned to call for help and then saw something that stunned her. Clunk moved with the speed of a cat, its movements as precise as a medtech surgeon android. The bot exploded toward the engine with the extension lever in hand. It slid on one knee to within inches of Brae's head, simultaneously positioning the extension lever beneath the engine near her neck. He lifted enough to free her leg, but just then the safety cable snapped, whipping wildly around to the bottom of the engine. The frayed end wrapped completely around Brae's outstretched leg, taut with unrelenting deadly tension. She screamed as metal strands tore into her leg. While keeping force on the extension lever to keep the engine from crushing Brae with one hand, the bot deftly reached with his other hand and snatched the cable that was threatening to sever her leg. Still trapped, Brae looked up at her mechanical savior. It turned its head downward, looking at her with eyes that seemed to hold a soul.

"I can hold this engine and cable for another 12.6 seconds. I recommend using the stasis field cutter beside you to cut the remaining cable," Clunk said with a smooth voice Brae had never heard before.

Brae grabbed the stasis cutter, switched it to full power, then set the edge against the cable wrapped around her leg. The cutter made quick work of the cable, releasing the death grip on her leg. Once free from the cable, Brae rolled out from under the engine just as Clunk let loose. It made a heavy "thunk" sound as it hit the floor. Brae reached for her leg, blood now freely flowing from the fresh wound, but at least her leg was still whole. She would need to stop the bleeding and soon. Before she knew it, Clunk had picked her up and began carrying her out of the repair shop and back to the house. She looked up at him, but he simply moved quickly without glancing her way. Once inside, the bot set her on the couch and retrieved a first aid kit and extra bandages, setting them beside Brae. It then went to the door as if to leave.

"Sit," Brae ordered.

The bot hesitated, then went to a chair in the corner of the room and sat down.

Brae worked quickly to clean and bandage the wound, stealing glances toward the bot every so often. She concluded that her wound was not a life-threatening injury, but that she should have a medtech check her over before too much time had passed. Once she was satisfied with the dressing, she stared across the room at the motionless bot. Clunk had just saved her life...twice.

What just happened? she asked herself, replaying every event that had taken place during the terrifying few seconds of the incident. A hundred thoughts and a dozen emotions flashed through her mind. She had known Clunk since she was a little girl. It simply wasn't capable of doing what it just did. Yet here she was...alive! Surely Dad had upgraded the bot with an entirely new processor.

"Explain to me how you were able to do that?" Brae asked the motionless bot.

"I do not understand," came the bot's delayed reply in its usual voice.

Brae eyed the machine through narrow eyes. "Have you been upgraded and are the other two bots like you?" she asked.

"I do not understand," Clunk repeated.

Brae smirked. She stood up and walked toward the bot, a limp now evident in her gait.

"Don't play stupid, Clunk, what is going on with you?" she demanded.

The bot continued to stare straight ahead as it had before. "I do not understand."

Brae found herself becoming angry. She glared at the bot then felt her leg starting to throb. She went back to the couch, elevated her leg on a footstool and continued to stare at the machine. Clearly, she would get no answers from the bot, so she waited. An hour later, Elias walked in the door and immediately knew that something was askew. The red-stained bandage on Brae's leg drew his attention first.

"Brae! Are you all right?" he asked, setting an arm full of supplies on the nearby counter. Moving quickly, he came and knelt down on the floor to inspect her leg.

"I'm fine," Brae said.

"We need to get you to a medtech," Elias said after taking a closer look at her leg.

"Not just yet," Brae replied, looking at Clunk out of the corner of her eye.

Elias caught the side glance and then saw the bot sitting motionless in the chair. He looked back at Brae. "What happened?"

Brae crossed her arms, giving the bot her full attention. "I was working on the S-23's left engine when the anti-grav hoist failed. Clunk here kept the engine from crushing me." Brae turned her attention back to Elias. "You mind telling me how that's possible?"

"I'm sure it just responded appropriately…giving aid when asked," Elias replied.

Brae frowned. "Yeah...I don't think so. It became a different bot, Dad. It moved like lightning then told me exactly what to do to survive the situation."

Elias looked toward the bot again. This time Clunk slowly turned its head to look at them. Shivers flitted up and down Brae's spine as the gaze of the bot revealed to her a presence she had never sensed before.

"She would have died...my liege."

Elias drew in a deep breath. "I understand. It's okay," he said, addressing the bot in a way Brae had never heard before. Elias looked back at Brae, taking a moment to look her leg over once more.

"Are you sure that doesn't need immediate treatment?"

"What's going on, Dad? What's the deal with Clunk?"

Elias took a seat next to Brae on the couch, gathering himself before speaking his next words.

"You'll understand when I tell you the end of the story. It's time."

Brae waited, wondering what about the story's end had to do with what had just happened.

CHAPTER

18

The Last Goodbye

Two more years passed, and Rayl truly began to feel like home to Daeson, Raviel, Tig, and Kyrah. Peace was fought for and won to a large extent. Daeson and Raviel's hearts filled with a contented gladness for the first time since Jypton. Tig and Kyrah's dream came true having established a home in a small country manor, and they all rejoiced greatly when Kyrah announced that they were to have a child in just a few months.

When Daeson and Raviel returned home that evening Raviel came to Daeson, a glimmer of hope and concern in her eyes.

"Do you think it's possible that this is the end of our calling as Navi?" Raviel asked. "We've seen so much, lived so much...I'm okay if this is it. It's what I've always dreamed of as a child and as a slave way back on Jypton."

Daeson wrapped his arms around her as they looked out on a beautiful Raylean sunset. He took a deep breath, wanting to say just the right words of assurance, but something in the corner of his mind unsettled him.

"We can hope so, Rav."

She pulled his arms tighter around herself, basking in the current peace of their lives. Then, she felt it. She peeled his arms away and stepped back.

"You know something, don't you?"

Daeson reached for her. "No...not really. I think it's just me being cautious." He then noticed a small crease in her brow.

"What is it, Rav?" he asked cautiously. "Are you slipping?"

Raviel bit her lip, returning to his arms. She looked up into his eyes.

"No, Daeson. I'm pregnant too."

Daeson froze. He instantly understood her apprehension. He opened his mouth to speak but the words would not come.

"I know," Raviel said. "I don't know how to process this either."

Slowly a smile spread across Daeson's face, and Raviel tilted her head quizzically.

"I know this could mean all sorts of things we can't even prepare for, but I can't help but love the thought of raising a child with you...our child!"

"Really?" she asked, her eyes lifting with delight.

"Yes...really. I love you, Raviel! We'll make this work. Somehow, we'll make this work."

Raviel rested her head on Daeson's chest. "Thank you," she whispered.

Six months later, Kyrah delivered a baby boy whom they named Kohen, for it was their heart to raise him up to always be a faithful follower of Ell Yon and to remember the legends of the Navi. There was an unspoken understanding what this would mean if Raviel were to experience a time slip event. After all, with Viper Two destroyed, there was only one Starcraft that was even capable of such a flight.

Three months later, when Raviel's time to deliver came, the pains of labor triggered the unthinkable. In a moment, Raviel was gone, leaving Daeson to cry out in anguish.

As tough as Raviel was, the pain of childbirth was something she couldn't seem to get on top of. It was a pain that swept her up and carried her wherever it wanted to take her. They'd had a plan with a medtech to manage the pain, for she knew what it might mean, but for some reason her contractions had come so quickly that there wasn't time to follow through.

Deep down inside her soul, Raviel knew that the spacetime anomaly was slowly destroying her. Each time it happened, another piece of her broke. And this time, the pregnancy seemed to magnify the impact on her body. She was tired. When she dissolved away from Daeson, an inexplicable cellular level pain surfaced that had not been there before. This time, the breaking seemed unfixable.

Daeson, please find me one more time, she begged. *Please Ell Yon...one more time.*

Daeson, Tig, Kyrah, and Rivet stood atop the hill overlooking Jalem. The remnants of the Navi Hall of Meditation were still evident as vestiges from an ancient time...a time they once called their own. This strange journey through time had been painful, challenging, thrilling and long. For this next jump Daeson would travel only with Rivet, leaving his friends behind forever. He first reached for Kyrah. He wrapped his arms around her, and she returned the hug firmly, seeming to struggle with what was about to happen.

"I wish I could see Kohen grow up," Daeson whispered. "You and Tig are going to be amazing parents."

"Please tell Raviel she was like a sister to me. I'll never forget her."

Daeson nodded. "I will," he said, pulling back and holding her at arm's length. "Be well, Kyrah, and may the greatest favor of Ell Yon be upon you, Tig, and your child."

Kyrah's tough eyes softened and threatened to spill tears. Daeson turned to Tig.

"It's hard to let you go it alone," Tig said, his eyes reddening.

Daeson pulled Tig into a strong embrace. "You've been more than a brother to me. There's only one Tig in the galaxy, and I've had the exclusive privilege to call him my friend. Thank you...thank you for everything!"

Tig pulled back, turning away to collect himself. Daeson had never seen tears in the man's eyes until now.

"I have something for you," Tig said, turning back to face Daeson.

He reached into his flight suit's breast pocket and removed a set of Raylean aerotech pilot wings. He snapped the wings in two and handed one half to Daeson. Daeson took the broken wing, looking curiously back at Tig.

"Though we part here and now, may we ever be joined in spirit and one day rejoin in the air as a flight of two once more," Tig said, his voice quavering.

Daeson grabbed Tig's hand and pulled him in again, reaching behind his neck with his left hand and leaning toward his friend until their foreheads met. Tig's parting actions and words had captured the spirit of their relationship in a timeless gesture of unbreakable friendship.

"And now I have something for you," Daeson said, reaching for the Protector on his arm.

Tig put his hand over Daeson's. "No. You need him."

"Ell Yon has been very clear. This Protector stays here...with you," Daeson returned. "You and Kyrah are Navi. I've passed on to you all that I know and have learned from the Commander. You must be the Keepers of the Protector, leading and guiding the people of Rayl."

Tig looked concerned. "I've never—"

Daeson put a hand on Tig's shoulder. "He's chosen you, Tig. It's okay."

Tig pursed his lips, nodding his acceptance. Daeson removed the Protector and pressed it onto Tig's forearm. After a few moments of recovery from Immortal revelation, Tig stood straight, eyes burning with the passion of Ell Yon. There were no more words to speak. Daeson looked once more at Tig and Kyrah, then turned to climb onto the ladder of his Starcraft. Rivet turned as well, but Tig reached for his arm.

"Be for him what I can no longer be."

Rivet paused, then lowered his head in acknowledgment. He turned his eyes to Kyrah.

"Be well, Lady Kyrah."

Kyrah smiled through her tears. "And you, my metal friend."

Within a few minutes, Daeson and Rivet were escaping the pull of Rayl's gravity as they broke orbit and prepared to launch into the future to find Raviel once again. Seconds later, they were gone, leaving Tig and Kyrah to live their long and fruitful lives in just a few short minutes.

Daeson wasn't prone to having anxious thoughts, but the knowledge that Raviel was suspended in time during her labor was more than he could take.

"Rivet, I need you to focus for me," Daeson said through the com mic. "Do you understand?"

"Perfectly, my liege. We must arrive in time to help lady Raviel. I understand your apprehension."

"Thank you, my friend."

Their flight took longer than the previous ones since an extra measure of caution was required to not overshoot Raviel's return to normal spacetime, and it worked. Daeson and Rivet arrived and caught Raviel just as she was resolving, 460 years later.

"Daeson!" Raviel screamed. "Don't let me go," she cried. "I can't anymore...I can't."

Although her labor was intense, Raviel remained present and gave birth to a healthy baby. When she was still weak with extreme fatigue four days later, Daeson sought the help of the best medtechs the present day could offer. Despite weeks of treatment and the best of their efforts, Raviel's strength would not return. Upon Raviel's insistence, Daeson dismissed the medtechs and took her to a small home in the country. Sorrow and joy jointly occupied Daeson's heart as he cared for Raviel and their child. Raviel nursed their baby girl, holding her every waking moment that she had the strength to do so. Daeson marveled at the selfless care of a mother for her infant, watching the beauty of unfathomable, life-giving love through the tenderness of Raviel.

"I want you to name her," Daeson said, embracing both child and mother.

Raviel kissed the little girl. "Not until I completely know her," she said with a gentle smile.

"Of course," Daeson replied.

For a few short weeks, they endured the fading of life together. Every day Daeson feared another time slip event was imminent, but one evening when Raviel seem saturated with fatigue, he carried her to her favorite place and sat her on the pillowed couch on their patio, their infant daughter asleep in a bassinet within arm's reach. Daeson sat next to her, and she leaned against his chest,

"Don't fear, Daeson. I'll not time slip again."

"How do you know, Rav?" Daeson asked, holding her close.

"Because my time has come."

Daeson's chest tightened inside, feeling her slump in his arms. He gently let her head fall to his lap. As he tenderly stroked her cheek, tears welled up. She looked up at him, eyes full of the deepest of love.

"I'll be waiting for you, my love," Raviel whispered as the light of life began to fade from her eyes...her beautiful eyes. Daeson bent forward resting his cheek next to hers. Her final whisper lighted on his ear.

"Her name is..."

With her final breath, Raviel gave their child her name, then closed her eyes forever.

Daeson's shoulders shook as he cradled Raviel in his arms. His tears spilled onto her paling cheek as he wept bitterly for his lost love. His mourning echoed through the ages touching the hearts of all who knew them. For many years his happiness had hung by a tenuous thread as Raviel skirted the ravages of her spacetime catastrophe. Too many times he had thought her lost only to discover she had fought through it...grasping tightly to the thread of life for his sake. But finally, that thread had snapped, and she was gone. He now joined hands with the ring of broken souls who yearned across the chasm of death for their lost soulmates. Was there any hope for such brokenness? Would joy ever be found in the heart of one so despaired? Daeson thought not. The cost was too great, the tearing too deep. With head and heart bent low, the muted calls for attention from their child were interrupted by a quiet familiar voice from his past.

"Daeson," the voice softly called.

When he refused to break from his inconsolable mourning, a gentle hand lighted on his shoulder.

"Daeson, your sorrow is but for a time. Take heart, Ell Yon is still with you both."

Daeson looked up. Lieutenant Ki stood before him as strong and as present as she had ever been. Beside her was another Malakian, eyes fierce blue reflecting the Immortal Ruah. He handed Lt. Ki a small, jeweled device, and she knelt beside Daeson. Carefully she placed the device on Raviel's forehead then pressed the center amber jewel.

"This is not for any human to see or know. Somehow, you have won exception with Ell Yon in order to ease your sorrow and strengthen you for the years to come. You have much to prepare," Lt. Ki said, stealing a glance toward the infant.

The amber jewel began to glow at the same time that six miniature mechanical tentacles gingerly propelled outward finding specific locations on Raviel's head. The light from the amber jewel intensified in a brilliant climax then diminished to a soft glow in a moment. The tentacles retracted, and Lt. Ki retrieved the device. She gazed into Daeson's eyes.

"You've done well, Servant of the Sovereign. Peace and rest are now yours for a season. Be well, friend."

Lt. Ki stood, reaching for the interphasal translator on her belt.

"I'm glad you're all right," Daeson said.

Lt. Ki nodded, then she and her companion were gone in an instant.

The cries of their child beckoned once more. Daeson gently laid Raviel from off his lap and went to the child. He picked up their baby girl in his arms and cradled her. The child peered out at him with dark captivating eyes. Daeson mustered a smile.

"You have your mother's eyes, little one." He reached and touched Raviel's still cheek. "Together we will remember her and honor her."

Elias lifted his head and looked into Brae's eyes. Tears welled up, threatening to spill as he reached for her hand. Despite all the doubts that had invaded her life over the past two years, Brae was taken once more with the story her father was telling. Just as if she was twelve years old again, the story became personal and real.

"What was her name, Dad?" Brae asked quietly.

Elias tried to smile, but as he did the unstoppable tears trickled down his cheeks.

"They named their baby girl, Brae." Elias's voice trembled with emotion.

Brae's eyes opened wide, her lips parting as she considered what her father was saying. An avalanche of confusing thoughts and emotions swallowed her mind.

"I don't think I—"

"You were that baby girl, Brae," Elias confirmed. "Raviel was your mother and I..."

Elias struggled. Brae pulled back, straightening her back.

"It can't be!" she exclaimed.

"Your name is Brae Starlore, and I am your father...Daeson Starlore."

Brae turned away, placing a hand on her head. She saw the bot still sitting silently in the chair...staring. She pointed.

"And that...that's..."

"Rivet," her father finished. "Please forgive me for not telling you until now, but there is a reason and purpose for it," he began to explain.

Brae looked back at her father. Had she been raised by a madman? This was so bizarre, especially now that she was coming to grips with what she currently believed about the galaxy and her people's history. She stood up and walked away, looking out to the country through the front window. Either her father was mad, she was mad, or the story he told was true. Logic allowed for no middle ground, and it frightened her.

"The Protector was clear. You weren't supposed to know until it was time," her father said as he stood.

Brae winced. Her father's stories were no longer just fanciful renditions of some legend, they were either indicators of insanity or threads of truth that were wrapped around every part of her life. She turned around to face her father. Beside him was the android. Her neck and arms tingled with chills as she looked at them.

"This is a little hard to believe, Dad. I just don't think—"

"I know," he interrupted. "Come with us."

Her father and the android moved toward the back door. She noticed that the bot's movements were perfect. Both it and her father stepped aside for Brae to walk past. They went back to the repair shop where her father briefly inspected the S-23 engine and the damaged hoist and safety cable. He glanced up at Brae, then to the android when he saw the crushed mechtech creeper and tools.

"Thank you," he said to the android. The bot simply nodded once.

Their interaction continued to stun Brae. Her father was reacting to Clunk as if he was a fellow human. It was odd.

"What are we doing here?" Brae asked.

Her father went to a power module on the wall, opened it, and pressed a recessed button that Brae had never noticed before. The sound of a large energy system powering up filled the room. A few seconds later, the floor beside them began to retreat away, the walls of the repair shop expanding outward as it did so. As the floor opened, soft warm lights turned on, illuminating the most remarkable sight Brae had ever seen. Twenty feet below them, the sleek form of an ancient war machine slowly came into view. It had the look of fierce power built into its design. Brae gawked in wonder as what she could only guess was a Jyptonian Starcraft from nearly 1500 years ago filled her view.

"I...I can't believe this!" Brae whispered. She looked up at her father. "I'm so sorry, Dad. I'm sorry I ever doubted you. It's just all so much to take in." She went to her father and leaned into him as he wrapped an arm around her shoulder, but it wasn't enough. She embraced him and he her. Brae stayed still for a long while, letting the impact of this colossal truth settle into her heart and mind while she healed in the loving arms of her father. Finally, she looked up into Daeson's eyes.

"My mother was truly Raviel?"

Daeson's eyes filled again.

"All this time you were telling me stories of my mother." Brae's eyes now filled with tears of her own. "Oh, Dad!" Brae buried her head into Daeson's chest.

"You're like her in so many ways," Daeson whispered.

After some time, Brae pulled away, wiping away her tears. She then went to Rivet and looked into his eyes.

"Thank you for saving my life, Rivet. As a little girl, I dreamed of having a friend like you, and you were right beside me all the time."

Rivet bowed his head. "It has been an honor to protect you, my lady. This was a command from Ell Yon himself."

Brae's eyes opened wide. She turned to look back at her father.

"What?" she exclaimed. "You said, 'until I was ready.' What does that mean, Dad?"

"Do you remember the oath Galec delivered to me centuries ago? In some mysterious way you are part of that oath. You're Brae Starlore, and Ell Yon wants you to be part of that legacy...a legacy that helps deliver hope to the Galaxy. Hope of the coming deliverance. There aren't many who are able to believe as we do."

Brae wondered at her father's words. How could she ever be part of something so important...so critical to the galaxy? Surely, he was mistaken.

Daeson glanced down at her leg. "Before we do anything else, let's make sure that leg of yours is okay."

Brae looked at the blood-soaked bandage, having completely forgotten her injury in the swell of such bizarre news. She looked down at the Starcraft once more, then to Rivet.

"What's next, Dad?"

"I'm not sure, Sweetheart. Only Ell Yon can answer that. In the meantime, you just keep being faithful," Daeson replied.

Brae nodded. There was a lot to process but returning home to the truth was sweet and reassuring.

"I can do that," she said with a broad smile. "I promise."

"The eyes of Ell Yon are upon all people, looking for one whose heart belongs wholly to him so that he can strongly support him...or her in the mission to which they are called." ~ Navi Daeson Starlore

Author's Commentary

The canvas of life upon which God has given us the ability to create story is truly remarkable—an undiscoverable universe, emotions, senses, a world of unrepeatable humans, and minds to think of untold adventures. My greatest concern regarding the writing of this series is in regard to my limited ability to appropriately represent the God of the Bible by the use of metaphors and allegory. Please do not make the mistake of assuming that science and technology can in some way explain away the supernatural marvels of God, His holiness, power, wisdom, and love. The full character of God is unknowable, and thus attempting to depict Him in all of His glory is a frightful endeavor. I pray that you return to His Word and fully embrace the profound descriptions of truth without fiction found there. It is my purpose in writing these words to point you once more to the glorious God of heaven and earth, His Son Jesus Christ, the Holy Spirit, and the radical intersection of supernatural love through the redemptive power of the gospel.

~Chuck Black

CPSIA information can be obtained
at www.ICGtesting.com
Printed in the USA
LVHW101554210422
716873LV00002B/94

9 781735 906171